ADVANCE PRAISE

"Texas is shaken by an apocalyptic flood in Kern's tense, entrancing debut novella. Noah, a trans man, takes refuge in a Dallas basketball arena-turned-relief shelter, rubbing shoulders with the full spectrum of Texas society, from members of the Austin queer community to conservative good ol' boys. Noah finds his place with Elena, a trans woman, and nonbinary Malone as the shelter residents band together in small groups to help one another. Noah is also visited by a ghostly boy, Abe, who he believes to be the spirit of his great grandfather, who delivers warnings and doles out advice. Noah struggles in a world without privacy, grapples with his complex relationship with his Jewish identity, and, as tensions rise between factions and conditions in the arena deteriorate, his loyalty to his newfound friends is tested. Noah faces the same choice his great-grandfather once wrestled with: to save himself or die helping his friends. With high stakes and a solid emotional core, and a perfect balance of speculation and an all-too-real vision of climate apocalypse, Kern shows the necessity of compassion, empathy, and community in the face of crisis."
★Publishers Weekly starred review

"*Depart, Depart!* grabbed me from its first, tense page. Noah's story of losing and finding community amid disaster, guided by the unreliable ghost of a traumatized ancestor, is too compelling to put down. Kern's writing is fierce and fearless, equally dextrous with portraying apocalyptic climate change or the joy of a queer dance floor when a DJ starts spinning Beyoncé. I'd say this novella isn't for the faint of heart, but it's for all of us trapped in unraveling situations, facing the seemingly intractable binary of being safe and alone, or vulnerable but together."
Nino Cipri, World Fantasy Award Finalist, and author of *Homesick* and *Finna*

Depart, Depart!

This is a work of fiction. All characters, organizations, and events portayed in this novella are either products of the author's imagination or are reproduced as fiction.

Depart, Depart!

Cover design by Anne Middleton

Edited by Selena Middleton

Published by Stelliform Press
Hamilton, Ontario, Canada
www.stelliform.press

Printed on 100% recycled paper

Library and Archives Canada Cataloguing in Publication
Title: Depart, depart! / Sim Kern.
Names: Kern, Sim, 1986- author.
Identifiers: Canadiana (print) 20200233327 | Canadiana (ebook) 20200233408 | ISBN 9781777091705 (softcover) | ISBN 9781777091712 (ebook)
Classification: LCC PS3611.E76 D47 2020 | DDC 813/.6—dc23

For all my family — blood and found

DEPART, DEPART!

Sim Kern

Stelliform Press
Hamilton, Ontario

A wave of humanity flows onto the court of the Dallas Mavericks basketball arena, wearing the clothes people wear at 3:00 AM, clutching the things people grab when they have seconds before the world ends. They streak mud across the rubber barrier protecting the court, dumping the backpacks and plastic bags and, in some cases, the nothing-at-all that is left of their lives onto army-green nylon cots. Families shout and wave to secure clumps of cots together. Chihuahuas and pit bulls strain at their leashes, snarling. The energy is blood-shot, the din panic.

Noah is rooted to the ground. For the last year, he's hardly left Montrose, Houston's queer neighborhood, where it's easy to forget that he lives in Texas. Now, hundreds of capital-T Texans swarm around him. They're busy scrambling for cots, but soon they will settle, and look around, and see Noah in their midst.

"You have to move," says the child staring up at Noah. He looks about seven years old. He's not transparent, but he *is* unpigmented, dressed in knickerbockers and a cuffed man's shirt, like an old-time black-and-white photograph made flesh. He has Noah's same long nose and black hair with a broad wave, and Noah strongly suspects that the boy is his great-grandfather Abe, at the age Abe was when his uncle stuffed him in a duffel bag and carried him onto a boat out of Germany.

Noah's not sure what he's more frightened of — Abe being real, or Abe *not* being real, or the thick-necked dad in a Texans jersey who just walked right through him. But the ghost boy

3

has saved Noah's life twice in as many days, so when Abe says, "Let's go," Noah follows.

Abe leads him off the court into the promenade, where more cots are lined up under darkened concession stands. It is quieter out here. A woman sits alone in an island of empty cots, near a single stall "family bathroom," and when Noah meets her eyes, they both smile, recognizing in each other an instant kind of home.

Elena is older than Noah — mid-forties, a dark-skinned Latina with thin hair pulled into a messy bun. She wears the polo shirt and khakis of a work uniform, but her sharply pointed manicure belies a different personal style. Incredibly, only one of the mustard-colored acrylics has ripped off, given ... well, what-ever her story is.

Noah's first impulse is to cling to Elena like a mother, but as he takes a step towards her, a family of five shoves him aside. Dad with shoulders like a bull, three white-blonde kids all in matching camo pajamas. The girl's are pink.

Fear submerges Noah's better impulses. Elena's smile fades. *Are* they safer together? Or more of a target? Noah looks around for Abe to tell him what to do, but the ghost boy is gone.

"Maybe we shouldn't —" Noah starts.

Elena tilts her head. As if she's read his mind, she says, "Under these lights? I'm not passing, and neither are you, honey." She pats the cot beside her. "Might as well stick together."

He drops to the cot, blushing at his hesitation. He does not take off his backpack. He thinks he might never take it off again.

Twenty-two hours ago, he boarded a bus at the Red Cross staging area in Conroe. He didn't manage to get much sleep on the interminable ride, stopping at every small town between Houston and Dallas, stalling in church parking lots until the driver would inevitably reboard and announce that every shelter in the area was full.

After the day-long ride, it feels amazing to be horizontal, but he can't close his eyes just yet. He scans the passing faces — wondering if that's Emeric with the undercut, or Sasha, beneath the floodwater-mucked hair? His heart skips a beat at certain older, white folks too, for that half-second before he realizes they're not his parents.

The cots around Noah and Elena remain empty for a long time. Maybe it's because folks don't want to sleep so near a bathroom. Maybe it's something else. Noah's never sure when to give people the benefit of the doubt.

Eventually, an older man with a shock of white hair stops in the aisle of flowing people. He's drowning in a baggy army jacket and hunched under the weight of an overstuffed camo backpack. His lip curls into a sneer, and there's no mistaking that look. Noah pretends to check the screen of his battery-dead phone, and the top of his head grows hot, as if the man's eyes are burning into him. It's maybe a full minute before the guy moves on.

"Isn't that incredible," Elena says, after the man disappears around the curve in the promenade, "that they can still find the energy to hate us, even with all this." She waves her hand elegantly.

A short while later, two white boomers in undershirts and boxers stop at the edge of the circle of empty cots. They bow their heads together, whisper-arguing in a way that suggests marital intimacy. The taller one clutches a tiny beast, which might be a Pomeranian under all that matted mud. He hisses something-something "privilege" and something-something "ally." The greying blonde thinks that a gathering of queers in this soup of humanity, all mixed-up, all separated from their bubbles of like-minded friends might be a bad idea. But the taller one persists, and eventually the other sighs, looking up at the promenade's high ceiling, where flags printed with the giant heads of the Dallas Mavericks look down on them like grinning gods.

David and Michael introduce themselves with bourgeois cheer, like new homeowners moving into a gated community, and claim the cots in front of Elena and Noah. The stream of humanity slows to a trickle, as the last of the cots are claimed. A few more queer-seeming people set down nearby. Two white women with a snarling Maine Coon in a cat carrier. A black woman with a taper fade takes the cot next to Elena's and promptly falls asleep beneath a mylar blanket. A 20-year-old who looks like an Instagram model spots Noah and blurts, "Thank fucking god, my *people!*" and dumps a few tote bags onto the cot next to Noah's. "Malone, they/them," they say, stretching out a hand.

Malone has a fall of black-to-seafoam hair and eyeliner that's miraculously unsmudged. By the end of the night, Noah will learn that Malone is nineteen years old, half-white, half-Vietnamese, their favorite band is the Coathangers, and they're pre-med at Houston Community College — planning to grow up to be an abortion provider.

For now, their outstretched wrist hovers in front of Noah, stacked with acrylic-bead bracelets in the colors of half-a-dozen queer flags, but Noah can't remember what any of them mean. It's been a day and a half since he woke up to the end of the world, and suddenly he can't remember who or what he's supposed to be, and why any of it ever mattered. "Sorry, I'm ... tired," he stammers.

"Hi, tired," Malone chirps, pumping his hand vigorously. Noah coughs a laugh, and it's a relief. He didn't know he was still capable of laughter.

"Sorry. I'm Noah," he says. "He/him."

"Oh my god, your name's really *Noah*?" They say with a wry grin. "That's a little on-the-nose, isn't it? This is all your fault, huh?"

🕊

Depart, Depart!

The first time Abe appeared to Noah was in a dream, in a dark and narrow stairwell. There are no stairwells in family stories about Abe, so Noah's subconscious must have borrowed from that stairwell up to the hidden annex, from Anne Frank's diary.

Abe stood a few stairs above Noah, his downturned face illuminated by a single candle. From the gloom below came a thundering that gradually resolved into distinct sounds — fists pounding on a door, dogs barking, and men shouting orders in German.

"It's time to go up the stairs," Abe whispered, eyes wide and urgent.

Noah woke with a choking feeling. Just another Nazis-at-the-door dream, he told himself. He'd had these nightmares since childhood, family stories merged with scenes from chapter books about the Holocaust. He forced himself to take slow, deep breaths, but the weight didn't leave his chest.

The streetlights had lost power, and no moonlight could penetrate the storm lashing the windows. It was so dark, it took his eyes a moment to notice the thickening of darkness above him. Then, a blaze of light from a match. Abe's face leaned close. Flecks of grime darkened the pigmentless cheeks.

"Up the stairs!" the boy hissed, then vanished.

Noah lay still, heart racing. Gradually, he realized the tight feeling in his chest was from falling asleep in his chest binder. He fished a hand under his sweatshirt and pulled the zipper down the middle, sucking in a grateful breath. The vision must have been sleep paralysis then, probably brought on by passing out in his binder, and the storm, and all of last night's tequila.

But then why did the smell of match-smoke linger in the air?

Noah crossed to the window and shined his phone's flashlight through the glass. The palms across the street strained sideways. Raindrops ricocheted so hard, it looked like they were falling upwards. But the street was only ponding at the margins — not even as bad yet as the Veteran's Day flood.

Out in the blazing-bright living room, Max and Sasha were still cuddled on the couch, legs entwined, watching anime on the big TV across a coffee table cluttered with beer cans and weed paraphernalia. At a tiny Ikea table, Emeric was drinking out of a red solo cup, watching the live stream of the Weather Channel on xer laptop.

"I can't believe you're all still up," Noah said.

"How can I go to bed when our intrepid hero Matt Smith is still out here, braving the elements?" Emeric had spent all night glued to the live stream for glimpses of the hunky meteorologist. Matt Smith wore a baseball helmet while reporting and did stunts like flinging bags of feathers in the air to show wind speeds. Before the storm made landfall, he was reporting from the beach, hunched over, shouting like the wind was about to bowl him over, while a couple strolled casually behind him, revealing the whole thing to be an act. Emeric was obsessed with him.

"What does Matt say about the storm?" Noah tried to sound casual, but the panicked feeling from his nightmare lingered.

"Martha's a Cat 4 now, so the worst should be over. But she's not moving North as fast as they thought. If she stays put over the city, we could flood almost as bad as during Harvey."

"You have overstayed your welcome, Bish!" Max called at the ceiling in his arch drag voice. "Move the fuck on."

"The street's starting to flood. I might try to move my car," Noah said, thinking aloud. Did *up the stairs* mean 'get to higher ground?' His gut told him yes. "The apartments down the street have that three-story garage. I'm gonna try to make it there."

"You're going out in this? *Alone*?" Sasha asked.

"I'll run back as soon as this band of rain passes." Noah pointed to the green tentacle sweeping through the satellite map on Emeric's screen. "Any of y'all want to come with me?"

8

"Ew, no. I'm way too cozy," Sasha said, snuggling her head into Max's chest. "Besides, the landlord says even during Harvey, our street didn't flood."

"What if this one's worse than Harvey?" Noah asked.

"First of all, my husband would never mislead us like that," Emeric said, slurring xer words. "Plus, Matt says the biggest danger is *wind,* so I don't know why you wanna go traipsing about outside. Seems like the top of a parking garage is the worst place to be, but ... you do you."

Noah wished he had Emeric's faith in the meteorologist, but every passing moment he spent in the ground-floor apartment was making his skin crawl. He didn't know how long he'd be stuck up on the parking garage, so he stuffed a few things in a plastic bag and zipped it into his backpack — his laptop and head-phones, a book, a bag of chips. Later, he would agonize over these hasty choices, wishing for all the things he didn't think to grab. His wallet. Clean underwear. His meds.

Maybe he left them behind because grabbing those things would've meant admitting to himself that he didn't think he was coming back. And if he didn't think he was coming back, he would've been morally obligated to drag his roommates out by the ankles, if that's what it took to get them to come with. He didn't. He didn't tell them about the ghost boy from the dream, or "get up the stairs," or his deep-down bad feeling.

Growing up, Noah always got teased for being a "scaredycat." He wouldn't jump off swings or go down the big tunnel slide, because there'd been a wasp in there once. In high school, he wouldn't ride rollercoasters, or try weed, or get in the car, that time Leanne wanted to drive home drunk from the homecoming bonfire. He insisted on calling his mom to pick them up, and Leanne never talked to him again.

Noah's dad always said this cautiousness was a Jewish thing, something to be proud of. Watching the Olympics, he'd scoff at the snowboarders flipping through the air. "Sports for gentiles," he'd say. Jews did not rock climb or ride motorcycles. "Your ancestors didn't escape the pogroms and the camps

9

for you to hold your life so cheaply." Noah hated when dad said stuff like that, hated it more when kids teased him for his own risk-aversion.

Maybe that's why he didn't tell his roommates that he had a terrible feeling about Hurricane Martha. Insisting they leave the comfort of the apartment for a cramped car on the rain-lashed roof of a parking garage — just on a *hunch* — would've been too much like something his dad would've done. Noah wanted to feel as brave and immortal as any gentile. He didn't want to spoil the party, lose his friends like he'd lost Leanne. He didn't want to be a coward.

So Noah stepped out into the rain and gusting darkness, closing the door on his roommates and the only family he could still call his own. Only later, lying on a cot in the Dallas Maverick's basketball arena, does he realize that nothing could have been more cowardly than his silence.

When Noah wakes, his left side is numb from the unforgiving nylon cot. Malone smiles in greeting, head hung upside-down, brushing out their long, damp hair with their fingers. Morning light streams in through the Promenade's high windows.

"They're serving breakfast by the south entrance. And they're letting people use the hot showers in the locker room. The lines are long, but it's worth it."

Noah sits up, sliding off his backpack and rolling out his tingling shoulder. His sweatshirt reeks of mildew, and his skin feels clammy. A shower would be amazing. "Single shower stalls or communal?"

"Both. They're taking turns letting in groups of men or women, and then you have to hurry if you want a stall, but — oh!" Malone holds a hand over their mouth, understanding. "I didn't even think about it ... I got in the women's line out of habit ..."

Noah looks down at his body and scratches his beard. The women's line is out of the question. But maybe he can get in the men's line and nab one of the single-stall showers in time. He pictures his body, naked behind a thin, vinyl curtain, in a shower room filled with so many hairy-backed Texas dads —

His vision blurs, and with a sickening lurch, he is not in the arena anymore, but inside a cinderblock chamber, each brick as stark white as Abe's skin. Showerheads hang from the ceiling, and grates are set high on the walls. He recognizes this place, from nightmares and history books. Across the room, Abe shakes his head so furiously that his skull blurs.

"No showers!" the ghost cries.

Noah blinks, and then he is back in the Mavericks' arena, splotches of light clearing from his vision. Malone frowns down at him with concern. Noah is concerned too. Abe has never sent him a vision that blocked out the whole world like that. Whether Noah is haunted or hallucinating, it's getting worse.

"I'll go with you," Malone offers. "To the showers? I'll find whoever's in charge. They should have considered the needs of trans people. I'm sure if I just explain —"

"Nuh-uh," Elena cuts in, neatly folding her mylar blanket. "Don't raise a fuss on our behalf, calling down all kinds of attention. Noah and I can wash up in there," she says, nodding to the door of the family bathroom. Noah mourns the loss of the anticipated hot shower, but he's not going to argue when Abe and Elena are in agreement.

Malone gives them the bag of travel soaps from the Red Cross, and Elena and Noah take turns trying to get clean in the small bathroom. Noah washes his hair in the sink, then scrubs his skin raw with a wad of paper towels. The faucet is on a five-second timer, so he has to wave his hand for each spurt of cold water. He tries not to catch his reflection in the mirror while his chest binder is off. He slept in it again last night, which he's not supposed to do — it's not good for his lungs or spine. The flesh-colored vest is ringed with pit stains and reeking of body odor. He considers washing it in the sink, but then what? He could let it dry over the baby-changing table, but what if someone grabs it or throws it out? And without it, he'll feel awful all day, tits hanging loose beneath his hoodie, reminding him with every step of their unwanted presence. He'll get that exposed feeling — like his clothes might as well be see-through — every time someone scans his chest to confirm their suspicions.

He forces himself to face the mirror then, trying to see what others see, what Elena saw when she said he couldn't pass "under these lights." After eight months on T, his jaw has filled out some, but his beard is still patchy fuzz that doesn't reach his cheeks. His lips might be a tell too. "Rosebud," his mother used to call them — a sharp Cupid's bow and a fat bottom lip. Not unthinkable that a cis boy would be born with those lips, but he'd probably get teased for them. It's why Noah chews his lips relentlessly.

Something funny happens to his vision then. The light in the bathroom flares, like an over-exposed Instagram filter. The fur on his cheeks vanish, the shadows of his features soften — just slightly — and then the face in the mirror is no longer Noah's, but *Nora's*.

Anger wells in Noah's chest. "Is this what you want from me?" he asks aloud. "You want me to be *her*?" But the ghost boy doesn't appear. Maybe it wasn't another vision, just exhaustion, with a side of dysphoria. Noah squeezes his eyes shut, and when he opens them again, the light has returned to normal.

It wouldn't take much. Shave his cheeks, take off the binder, maybe trade his hoodie for a cardigan, and he'd clock as female again. Would it be so terrible — to let other people *ma'am* him, to keep things simple during a crisis?

And yet, the thought of it makes Noah feel like the ground has fallen away, like he's slipping beneath dark water. He hurries back into his binder, relaxing only once he's zipped in its snug embrace. He pulls on the loose jeans and oversized hoodie that hide his curves, the fabric still reeking of mildew. In the mirror is a slight man with a peach-fuzz beard and rose-bud lips. It might be a liability, but it's a face he recognizes as his own.

The rest of that first day involves lots of waiting in lines. There are lines to get food, and lines to charge your phone, and lines to sift through tables mounded with donated clothes. Noah finds another pair of jeans that are roughly his size and some T-shirts, the necklines stretched, the cheap cotton stiff from over-washing. Back at the cots, Elena looks more herself, in skinny jeans and a purple top with a ruffle around the chest. She shows him a couple of thick, XL sports bras she grabbed from the women's donations.

"I saw you wear a binder, and I was thinking you could layer these up when you want to give it a rest?"

Noah stares down at them in silence, wondering how she knew.

"If you don't want them, I can use them —"

"No, I do. Thank you," Noah whispers, hoarse from pushing words past the lump in his throat. He folds the bras and stuffs them into his backpack.

"They've set up a medical clinic in the administrative offices," she says. "You're on T, right?"

Noah nods, but his pulse races at the thought of seeing a doctor here. "I'm guessing it's not that kind of clinic ..."

"But we can try," Elena says, slinging a rumpled suede bag over one shoulder.

The line for the clinic stretches halfway down the stairs up to the administrative offices. Elena and Noah stand together, ignoring everyone else's eyes. Noah can never be sure whether someone is staring *at* him or in his general direction, whether a squint is hostile or merely curious, whether he's being naive or paranoid — and it's exhausting to try. He starts feeling a familiar guilt, for taking up space in this line filled with sniffling-coughing people, for existing in a way that's so bothersome to others.

Elena tries to make small talk, but they have little in common, besides the obvious. They've never heard of each other's favorite bands. Elena likes hip hop and Tejano, while Noah mostly listens to indie rock. Elena's favorite movie is *To Wong Foo*, which Noah's never seen, and his favorite show is *Steven Universe*, which she's never seen. Their conversation is punctuated with awkward silences. But when the nurse finally calls their names, Elena squeezes Noah's hand, and he knows she understands him in the ways that matter most.

Several different doctors are seeing patients inside a row of curtained-off cubicles. Noah groans inwardly when the nurse pushes back a curtain to reveal an older white man. The doctor takes the clipboard from Noah's hand without looking up.

"What's wrong with you?" he asks flipping through the paperwork.

"Uh, nothing. I mean, I'm not sick. I'm, uh," Noah tries to muster some pride in his voice. He has every right to be here, seeking care. "I'm transgender."

The doctor looks up then. Clocks Noah's facial hair. His chest. Flicks to his crotch. Back to his face.

"You know, when you fill out medical paperwork, you should indicate your *sex,*" the doctor says, "so you can be treated appropriately."

Noah tries to hold his voice steady. "I just need a prescription for testosterone."

"Look, I'm not a psychiatrist. I don't treat people with your ... condition. And there's a lot of sick people here, who need actual medical care."

Roiling with shame, and shame for *feeling* shame, Noah mumbles an apology and bolts from the cubicle. Elena waits at the edge of the curtained row. Her chin is held high, but her eyes are rimmed in red.

"You shouldn't have apologized," she says, as they head down the stairs. "You've got nothing to be sorry for."

"I know that, but it's like a reflex."

She sighs. "Yeah, I know. I get it. My doctor said, 'We're only addressing high-priority needs right now,' I was like, 'Bitch, in the time it took you to say "high-priority needs" you could've written me a script for E. It's not hard.'"

"Did you say that?" Noah asks.

"No," she snorts, and they fall silent for several stairs. "What happens when you stop? Will your beard fall out?"

"I don't think so, but it'll stop growing in. And my period will come back after a while. Mostly, I'll just feel *wrong* I guess."

"Yeah," Elena says, rubbing her jawline like it already prickles. "Well for what it's worth, I think you're a 'high-priority need,' and we'll figure out something, together."

Later, Noah sits against the promenade wall, waiting for his laptop and phone to charge. As soon as his computer boots up, he "checks himself safe" from Martha on Facebook, then scans the list of friends who have done the same, heart in his throat. He sees a few kids he went to high school with — the ones he didn't block before coming out — some college friends, his shift manager at Drip Drop ... But Emeric, Max, and Sasha are not on the list.

He checks their individual pages, but none of them have posted anything since the early hours of the storm. Emeric's last post was a gif of Matt Smith tripping dramatically in four inches of floodwater, captioned, "Iconic. We must stan."

Noah sends them each a direct message — *I got evac'd to Dallas. At the Mavericks' arena. Are you okay?* He stares at the Messenger windows for a long time, but the "typing" bubbles never appear.

Half a dozen times, he starts a similar email to his parents, then deletes the draft. It's been six months since he's talked to either of them — since shortly after he told them his real name. He chose Noah, in part, because it was a "good Jewish name," and so close to the one they gave him. He thought that would make it easier for them.

When he came out, they didn't yell or kick him out or anything. But they kept calling him Nora and using female pronouns for months, not even making an effort. His mom started following TERFs on Facebook — forwarding him graphics about the dangers of taking testosterone and articles about "radical trans brainwashing" in the media. Eventually, he stopped answering when they called.

But his parents live (lived?) in Bellaire, which floods even in a sun-shower. Noah is gripped by a sudden, visceral memory of a lazy high-school afternoon, lounging at the kitchen counter with mom, during their "girl time," as mom called it, before dad got home from work. They'd gossip about kids at school and relatives, while Nora painted his nails black, and the smell of baking challah wafted from the oven.

Tragedies make people realize what's really important, right?

Before he can overthink it, he hits "send" on the email to his parents.

Next he checks the news, but the anchor is standing in front of a hologram of the Addicks dam, explaining that

Houston is — *was?* — a city scooped out of mucky, coastal prairie — its dry land artificially maintained by a network of concrete bayous and two massive dams to the west — the Addicks and Barker. The Addicks dam had held two hundred million cubic meters of water back from the city until Martha had overfilled it, and its walls had crumbled. The ticker at the newscaster's feet reads, "Dam Collapse: Death Toll Estimated in the 100,000's." Panic claws up his throat, and he slams the laptop shut.

The other people gathered around the tangle of power-strips are all on the phone with insurance companies or assuring relatives that they're doing fine. But Noah has no one to call. He's not a homeowner, and his friends and family are probably —

But he doesn't want to think about that.

So he turns his mind to Abe instead, wondering what these visions might mean. Noah majored in psychology in college, and he has a hunch Abe is some kind of stress-induced hallucination. The diagnosis is not comforting, because these symptoms could indicate the onset of schizophrenia, which tends to manifest at Noah's age. So far, Abe seems to be a survival mechanism — a manifestation of Noah's fears and gut instincts — that has served Noah well. But there's no telling if these visions will subside with the floodwaters or mark the on-set of a lifetime of delusion.

Noah was raised in a family of proud atheists, so he doesn't let himself seriously consider alternative explanations. Earlier, in the bathroom — when he tried to talk to Abe aloud — that was simply a moment of panic, brought on by gender dysphoria and stress.

There's no such thing as god or ghosts. No life after death.

When Noah gets back to the cots, he spots new faces. Malone met some queer college kids in the food line, and they've moved their stuff nearby. After everyone introduces themselves and their pronouns, Elena jokes that their part of the arena should be called "Montrose Dos," after Houston's queer neighborhood, and they all laugh.

"I was in Montrose, you know, when the dam broke," Noah says. Everyone falls silent. Instantly, he regrets saying anything, spoiling the moment.

How? Malone mouths, eyes wide. They mean, how did you live to tell about it? Everyone's seen the footage, the wall of water that claimed every neighborhood from the beltway to downtown.

"You know those apartments at Studemont and Allen Parkway? I was in my car, on top of the parking garage."

They wait for him to say more. He looks down at the cot, because it's easier than meeting their eyes.

"It wasn't like it looks on TV. There wasn't this huge wave or anything. From the top of the garage, I could see Buffalo Bayou, and it was out of its banks already, but it always does that in a bad storm. And then all of a sudden it started coming up. Just," He lifts his hands to show the speed of the rise. "You know how the old Party Boy warehouse is right there? I watched the water go up the side of the building. One story, two stories. On top of the parking garage, there was like, this little shed — or I guess it was the entrance to the stairwell. The roof there was a little higher than the cars, and I got a feeling that I had to get up there."

He doesn't share that "the feeling" was a ghost boy banging on his rain-lashed car window, shouting, "Up the stairs!"

"So I got out of my car, and I climbed up on a truck to get on that roof. And it was just in time, because then I heard this sound, like —" He shakes his head, searching for words. "— like a million rolls of thunder all at once. Then the water came over the top of the garage and it pushed the cars — *my* car, where I'd been sitting a second ago — it pushed them clear off the roof, like they were rubber duckies. And I could see how fast the water was moving because of all the stuff in it. Parts of houses and roofs and cars, and —"

His voice breaks, and he stares down at his lap, filled with the sudden certainty that his messages to Emric, Max, and Sasha will remain unread. The water came up so fast. There was no way they'd gotten out in time. With terrible clarity, he sees a vision of his friends' bodies, drifting through the darkened, flooded tomb of their apartment.

Malone rests a hand on his back, bringing him back to the present moment.

"After a while the water started going down. I guess the dam had emptied out by then. I kept hoping to see buildings or lights out where Montrose was, but it was all dark. It just rained and rained, until I thought my skin was gonna dissolve. I thought that was it for me, you know? And I really don't know if it was twenty minutes or hours — but finally a helicopter came."

There's a long silence.

"I was North of 610, where it wasn't so bad," Malone breathes.

"I was in Katy," Elena nods. "Got stuck at work and the Cajun Navy rescued me off the roof of the Dollar Tree. But the water wasn't more than three, four feet deep there." She clears her throat. "I had a lot of friends in Montrose."

"We all did," David says, voice rasping.

"We've had bad storms before, right?" Malone says. "Hurricane Harvey, Ike … and New Orleans came back from Katrina."

"I think this time is different." Noah says. He presses his fists to his eyes to blot his tears. In the darkness behind his eyelids, he sees swift, dark water.

Noah knows two stories about his great-grandfather Abe. The first is the business with the duffel bag. He's always pictured it as stiff, green canvas. Airholes disguised as punctures from normal wear and tear. He doesn't know the details, just that three-line story. "He got in the duffel bag. His uncle carried him onto the boat. The rest of the family went to the gas at Dachau."

Only now does Noah realize that the story begs a million questions. Did Abe cry when he said goodbye to his family? Was it his choice or did his parents force him in the bag? Was Abe stuffed in the cargo hold — forced to hide in the bag the whole voyage? Or was he able to get out once on board and mix with the other kids? That seemed more likely. But what did they eat? And did he get seasick? And how did he pass the time?

Noah never asked his dad these questions, and now he may never get the chance. By the dimming of the lights on their second night in the arena, neither of his parents have responded to his email. There could be other reasons for this, but it seems grotesque that they would matter.

Noah suspects his dad might not know the answers, anyway. Information on Abe is limited because of the second story Noah knows about him. Noah's dad always told it like this:

"When I was six or seven years old, my dad took me into a cigar shop. This old guy came in, real down on his luck, maybe homeless. Dad was holding my hand, and I felt his grip tighten. The old guy stared at my dad and said, 'Your face is familiar, but I can't quite place you.'

"My dad said, 'It's me. It's Herschel.' And the guy looked just ... stricken. He said, 'I'm sorry. I didn't recognize you.' Then my dad paid, and we walked out of the store, and about halfway down the block, my dad said, 'That was your grandfather. That was Abe.'"

See, the boy in the duffel bag grew up to be a lying, gambling schmuck who ran out on his family when his son Herschel was fourteen years old. This was back when most women didn't work outside the home, so Herschel had to drop out of high school to take care of his mother and sisters. He only saw his father once after that — twenty years later, in a chance encounter in a cigar shop. And so, Abe's name had always been spat like a curse in Noah's family.

Maybe it's because he keeps seeing his boyhood ghost, but Noah feels more empathy for Abe than his father or grandfather ever showed. Abe must have carried that duffel bag for the rest of his life, carried inside it the terror of exile, the loss of his homeland, the murders of his parents and siblings and everyone he'd ever known, all "gone to the gas" at Dachau. Even settled in sunny, oil-rich Houston, with baby Herschel on his lap, Abe's heart must have stopped at every foot on the stairs, every knock at the door.

On the second morning in the arena, the population of Montrose Dos waits in line for sausage and scrambled eggs. "You would think, considering climate change is ultimately the reason we're here, that they would provide a vegan option," Malone says. "Or at least reusable cutlery."

A skyscraper of water-bottle pallets looms over the tables of volunteers, all wearing plastic gloves to scoop food onto the Styrofoam trays that are overflowing in all the garbage cans scattered around the arena.

"You're vegan?" Agatha asks, arching an eyebrow at Malone. She's the short-haired black woman who sleeps beside Elena. She wears a blazer over her T-shirt, and the cut of her jacket is remarkably sharp for something scrounged out of a donation pile.

Malone shrugs. "Freegan, I guess, 'cause I'm gonna eat all of that."

"Same," Agatha sighs.

In front of them, a mom on the phone shouts, "File a claim! Speak to a representative!" A toddler tugs on her arm, whining "I'm hun-ry!" and two older kids fight over a Nintendo Switch.

Agatha bends at the waist and says in a booming, cheery voice, "Hey, kids, let's let your momma talk on the phone, huh?" She's caught the little one's attention. "Let me guess, do you like that baby shark song?" The toddler nods. "Now I don't think I remember all the words." Agatha turns to the older siblings. "Can you two help me sing that shark song, so your momma can make her phone call?"

"I guess," the oldest boy says. He turns to his little sibling and makes his fingers into pincers. "*Baby shark doo doo ...*"

The kids start singing, and Agatha joins in. To make the mommy shark, they hold their wrists together while their palms clap. Then it's the daddy shark's turn, and he's exponentially larger — his mouth formed by the whole of their arms, his jaws as wide as their shoulders. It's a tidy song for teaching all kinds of things about how families and genders are supposed to work.

Malone leans into Noah's ear, "*Nonnnnn-binary octopus doo doo,*" they whisper, waving their arms like noodles. Noah laughs, but part of him is annoyed by this reminder of their otherness — how neither of them belong inside the neat constructs of children's songs.

"All these parents need childcare," Agatha says, now that the kids are engrossed in the song. "They have to make FEMA claims and deal with all that mess." Throughout the arena, children tug on their parents, fight with each other, jump between cots, or stare into tablets and phone screens. "And these kids have been through trauma. They could use some routine and structure. They could use school."

"What, are you a teacher or something?" Noah asks.

"A principal, actually." Craning her neck, she narrows her eyes at a clump of lounging teenagers high up in the stands.

Depart, Depart!

After breakfast at the cots, Agatha disappears, and Michael and David go somewhere to work on their insurance claims. Noah scrounges a deck of cards and plays Egyptian rat screw with Malone and the college kids for hours. It gives him a dreamy, nostalgic feeling, like they're a bunch of kids and Elena is their camp counselor, and they're all waiting around for their parents to pick them up.

Agatha returns at lunchtime. She's convinced the arena owners to let her use the corporate suites as classrooms, and she's wrestled up enough certified teachers among the refugees to run a half-day school and daycare, for any parents who need it.

"You made a school? Just like that?" Malone says in awe.

"That's my girl!" Elena squeezes Agatha's arm. The two of them are the only 40-somethings in Montrose Dos, and they've made fast friends.

"Right, well, time to get off your butts and help out," Agatha says. She hands them a stack of flyers to tape up around the arena. "We need all the supplies on this list." She hands them a printout. "See if you can find people to donate this stuff."

"Ooh, I bet I can get this crowdfunded," Malone says. "Everyone on my Twitter feed has been asking how they can help us. Some of the Dallas folk have even offered to drive stuff over." They bow their head to their phone, thumbs already flying.

"Wonderful," Agatha says. "How long will that take?"

"I bet we can get this stuff donated in a day or two."

"Then Noah, can I put you in charge of asking around to see if anyone can lend us these things?" She circles the first ten items on the list. "These are our most urgent needs."

"Noise-cancelling headphones?" He reads aloud. "What, some kid has an urgent need for Beats by Dre?"

Agatha looks unamused. "There's a boy here with autism who's sensitive to noise. This place is basically his worst nightmare."

23

Noah's cheeks burn with embarrassment. The cacophony of the arena swells in his ears, like someone's turned the volume up — kids screaming, dogs barking from the kennels. The din of a thousand voices.

"I'll find you headphones," he says.

But as he walks away from Agatha, clutching the list of supplies, his stomach churns with a deepening sense of dread. He's spent the last few days trying to interact with people outside Montrose Dos as little as possible. Now he's agreed to walk up to strangers and ask them to lend him one of the few possessions they have left in the world.

There's plenty of people wearing earbuds along the promenade, but not the noise-cancelling kind. The first woman he sees with bulky, promising-looking headphones has too much Aqua Net in her hair for Noah to feel safe approaching her. On the court, he spots some expensive headphones, but they're wrapped around the bald head of a white dad with the build of an ex-high-school-fullback. Noah gives him a wide berth and heads up into the stands.

A group of black teenagers are hanging out about halfway up the first section of seats, and one of them has a trendy pair of headphones slung around his neck. Noah deeply doesn't want to talk to them either. They're having a nice time, off by themselves. They don't want to be interrupted by some white grown-up, asking for their stuff. But if he doesn't talk to *them* because he's afraid — well, what does that say about him?

So Noah forces his feet up the stairs, heart pounding in his throat. He slouches deeper, caving his chest to hide the bulge beneath his binder.

As he reaches their row, someone says something funny, and the teens all burst into laughter. He takes a few steps closer, and they knit their eyebrows at him.

"Uh, hi." He clears his throat, dropping his voice to a lower pitch. He was a soprano to begin with, and his voice hasn't dropped as much as he'd hoped when he started T. "So, my friend Agatha is starting a school here? She's trying to find

24

these things." Staring down at the typed sheet of paper, he explains about the kid who's stressed out by loud noises.

"No shit? I got a nephew with Asperger's," the guy wearing headphones says.

"They don't call it that anymore, Damien," says a girl with silver box braids. "You're supposed to just say 'autism' now."

Damien holds up his hands, "Okay Kayla. Tell that to his mom."

Kayla sucks her teeth, "Don't get defensive, just adjust your vocabulary."

Noah clears his throat again, "So, um, we're seeing if any-one has noise-cancelling headphones he can borrow — for a day or two until we can get some donated."

"Ohhhh, I see what this is." Damien jumps out of his seat and puffs out his chest. "You trying to steal my headphones, white boy?"

Noah flinches back. The teens all bust out laughing.

"I'm just playing with you," Damien says, grinning and dropping the pose.

"Hoooo, you should've seen your face," Kayla laughs.

Noah blushes, but he doesn't mind their teasing. Damien called him "white *boy*." Even though, according to Elena, he doesn't pass "under these lights."

"For real, though," Damien says. "I'd totally help, but these are knockoffs. You can have them, but they're not noise-cancelling."

"Lemme see that list," Kayla says, grabbing the paper from Noah. "Diaper rash cream, hand sanitizer, picture books, crayons ... Hey, you want help finding this stuff?"

"Yeah, uh, that would be great."

"Let's go." She whacks the sneakers of the girl lounging with her feet up in the row above. "C'mon it'll be like an Easter egg hunt. Can I keep this?" she asks, holding up the paper.

"Sure," he says.

When they get to the court, the teens fan out, some of them heading to the promenade. Damien sucks in a lungful of air and shouts, "Yo, listen up! Some teachers starting a school up in here, and they need y'all to help out with donations. Any of you got some —" He holds up a finger for each item on the list. "— diaper rash cream, hand sanitizer, crayons ..."

When Damien first started shouting, some people had looked startled, even scared or mad, but as he continues, their faces relax into relieved smiles. By the time he's finished, a crowd has gathered — all kinds of people, all eager to donate one of the few things they have left in the world.

Noah holds out the bottom of his hoodie to make a basket for carrying all the donations. One girl, maybe eight years old, insists Damien take her doll, "For some little kid that don't got toys." She won't take no for an answer, and Damien reverently promises to find a good friend for the doll.

Noah, Kayla, and Damien spend the rest of the afternoon collecting donations and ferrying them up to "Miss Agatha." Down on the court and the promenade, it's like the whole arena has mobilized to get the school up and running. Malone has been tweeting like mad, and their kickstarter has raised $500. Someone even dropped off a bunch of indoor playground equipment, and a group of dads are setting it up on the second-floor promenade, looking as cheerful and ethnically diverse as a holiday Gap ad.

Noah wonders if Agatha didn't know they needed this — a sense of purpose, a shared project — the same way she knew that mom in line needed her to sing Baby Shark to the kids.

He's heading back upstairs to see what else he can do to help, when a heavy hand clamps his shoulder from behind. He spins and finds himself staring up into the face of the football dad he'd spotted earlier. His guts turn to water.

"You're with that schoolteacher, right?" the man drawls in a thick Beaumont accent — that swirl of Lou-zee-anna Cajun and a Texan drawl. He holds out his expensive headphones. "Someone said there's a kid who needs these more'n I do."

"Wow," Noah says, taking the headphones. "Thank you so much. I — I'll get these back to you as soon as we get another pair donated."

"Keep 'em as long as you need."

Now that Noah looks closely, he sees the gentleness in the man's eyes and the laugh lines surrounding them.

Noah drops the headphones off with Agatha and takes the steps back down to the court two at a time. His heart feels almost okay. There's still grief and terror at the edges of his mind, lurking outside the flimsy soap bubble of the present moment. But when he thinks about today, the way everyone came together, all different ages, races, ethnicities, in a beautiful testament to the human spirit —

A shriek rends the air. Then dozens of voices are screaming, then hundreds. On the court below, people are running, charging the doors to the promenade, jamming into the player entrances. More people stream around them, jump into the stands, running up the stairs to where Noah stands frozen, his eyes searching for the source of the panic.

"Get down!" comes a familiar child's voice. Abe is crouched behind a row of bleachers. He reaches up to tug Noah's wrist, and it feels like an icy wind catching his sleeve. Noah lets the ghost boy drag him to the earth as the stampede of people reaches him and heads up towards the second level.

Abe's face is very close to Noah's, and the child's eyes are wide with fear. He points through the gap in the seats onto the empty court. Amid the trampled possessions and overturned cots stands a single man. Noah recognizes that shock of white hair, the baggy army jacket. It's the old man who'd glared at him with so much hatred that first night in the arena.

And he's holding an AR-15.

"It's just a rifle, people, calm down!" The man cackles in amusement, watching the stragglers who are still trying to shove into the promenade.

The crowd around the northern entrance gives way, and a half-dozen cops emerge onto the court, walking slow, hands at their belts.

"Sir, put the gun down," orders a bald, white cop.

"I know my rights! The law says I can open carry my own rifle."

"True, true. But this is private property, sir," the cop says, "and the arena owners do not allow open carry here."

"House Bill 1177 states the right to carry a legally-owned firearm even in a mandatory evacuation," the man rattles off, clearly rehearsed. The cops on the court fan out in a semi-circle. High up in the stands, more cops file down the rows of seats, carrying long, thin guns. Noah presses his stomach to the cold cement and tries not to imagine bullets ripping through the skin of his back.

"That is right, that is the law, and you know I'm here to uphold the laws, don't you sir?" says the cop, touching his chest with a splayed hand. "We're on the same side."

"Then why're you trying to take my rifle?" The man swings the barrel to gesture, and half the cops jump back. "This is my god-given, second-amendment right!"

"Because we've got a term for what's happening here, and that's called 'inducing a panic.' It's a misdemeanor," the cop says. "But as far as I'm concerned this is a mis*understanding*. Just put your rifle down, and we can talk. No one has to get arrested."

The man looks around, noticing the semi-circle of cops surrounding him. His eyes flick to the trained barrels in the stands high above. He and the bald cop mumble to each other, too softly for Noah to hear. Then, gently, he sets the rifle on a cot and holds up his hands. The bald cop grabs the gun, and another cop rushes forward, twisting the gunman's arms behind his back.

"Hey, I thought you said — !"

"We're just going somewhere to talk," the officer assures him.

28

Depart, Depart!

"This is bullshit!" the gunman roars. "You think *they* don't have guns? You lock us up in here, with all these"— and he rattles off a string of racist and ethnic slurs, and the slur that Noah has heard, shouted at him out of car windows — "and these f*****s! I got a right to protect myself!"

As the police escort the raving gunman off the court, Noah lets out the sob he's been holding back. It was undeniably brave, the way that cop walked towards the barrel of the gun. Noah doesn't delude himself that he has anywhere near that level of courage, and he feels a dizzying sense of gratitude towards the police. But it makes him feel sick too, the way the cop acted like he was on the gunman's side. Noah hopes that was just an act — a successful one, because the situation ended bloodlessly. But he can't shake the conviction that if Damien had been holding the gun, things would've gone very differently.

Gradually, people re-emerge onto the court and start straightening cots and collecting their scattered belongings. Their voices are different now. They are sucking down gulps of air, holding each other, crying. A few nights ago, they all lost their homes, their city, and many of the people who gave their lives meaning. Now even the puny sense of security afforded by this shelter has been stripped away.

Noah heads back up the stands towards Agatha's school. As soon as the commotion started, she'd herded all the kids into the windowless hallway behind the suites. Here, the last few kids are sniffling together, waiting for their parents to collect them.

"Can I do anything to help?" Noah asks. Agatha shows him to a cabinet with cleaning supplies and asks him to wipe down the tables and doorknobs with disinfectant. Having a job to do steadies him, though that expansive, magnanimous feeling from earlier in the day is long gone. When he finishes, he empties all the wastebaskets into one garbage bag. Agatha approaches as he's tying off the knot.

"Are you okay?" she asks.

A cascade of images crashes through his mind. The gunman screaming slurs. Noah's inbox, empty of messages from his parents or friends. Dark water rising, his apartment filling — too fast for Emeric, Max, and Sasha to get out.

"No," he says, tears leaking down his cheeks. "Are you?"

She shakes her head. "My girlfriend lives in Montrose. I wanted her to stay with me during the storm, but she didn't want to leave her cats." Her voice breaks on the last word, and she shakes her head furiously. After a moment of fighting off tears, she adds, "I'm allergic."

"Oh god. Oh, I'm so sorry," Noah whispers. "No one knew what was going to happen. It's not your fault." He doubts that Agatha believes him, not when his own survivor's guilt is eating him alive.

Agatha nods, wiping her eyes with the back of her hand. "Ugh. That awful little man got to me."

Noah wonders if she could hear what the gunman was shouting from the hallway. He hopes not. "At least he's gone now, right? We're safe."

She cocks her head and shoots him a teacher-look, like when a student gives an answer that's *almost* right, but also miles away.

"Would you like to come back and help out here tomorrow? We could use a teacher's aide in some of the classrooms. I think Kayla and Damien are going to volunteer."

Noah's vision blurs, and with that sickening lurch, he realizes the world is falling away again. Everything tilts, like he's on a carnival ride, and then he's slammed down onto a cobbled street, devoid of color. The shadows cast by the buildings are made of tiny dots, like this world is a xerox of a xerox of a picture in a book. A few paces ahead, Abe sits on the stairs of a narrow building, playing with a cup-and-ball toy.

"Not again," Noah groans aloud. His words sound fuzzy and distant, as if there's not enough air in the vision to carry his voice. "Who are you?" he asks louder. "Are you Abe? My great-grandfather?"

The boy nods but doesn't look up from his toy.

"Why are you showing me this?" Noah demands. Abe looks away from him — up the street — to where two figures are coming down the narrow sidewalk. The woman's blonde hair is pinned beneath the kind of delicate hat that was fashionable a century ago. The girl clutching her hand has the same white-blonde hair, set in rag curls. The mother spots Abe and presses the girl's head into her skirt, steering her across the empty street.

With a *chunk!* the ball on the string lands in the cup. Abe stares meaningfully at Noah.

Then Noah is back in the arena, slumped against the wall. Agatha leans over him, eyes knit with concern. "Are you okay? I think you fainted."

Noah nods slowly, his head pounding where it must've slammed against the wall. Fainted? He's never fainted in his life.

"You were mumbling something — I couldn't make it out."

"I'm fine. Sorry. Just got dizzy all of a sudden."

"It's been a terrible day. Days, actually." She reaches down a hand and helps him to his feet. "Drink some water when you get downstairs, okay?" Noah nods and turns to head back down to the court.

"Oh —" she calls after him. "You never answered, though. If you're feeling better tomorrow, do you want to come and help the teachers?"

Suddenly Noah understands why Abe showed him what he did. The way that gentile woman steered her child across the street, at the sight of a certain kind of boy. Here in the arena, it's probably not Noah's *Jewishness* that parents will mind, but some of them will see him with the same kind of fear.

"I don't think that's a good idea," he says, and he turns to head back to the court.

🕊

Back at Montrose Dos, Malone pulls Noah into a long hug. They trade stories of what-they've-heard, and Noah learns that the gunman's name is Roger Thibodeaux, and that all this time he's been carrying that AR-15 in pieces inside his backpack, and that at around 5:00 PM today he huddled under a mylar blanket and assembled it smack in the middle of the basketball court.

Malone sits on their cot, furiously coloring a rainbow flag onto a sheet of computer paper, using crayons from a box of donated art supplies.

"— all of a sudden, hundreds of people came running off the court. They were trying to get out this entrance, but you know those doors are kept locked."

"It was wild," Elena nods. "Folks were smashing each other into the doors and pounding on the glass. We headed to the north doors, which are usually open, but there were all these cops coming in."

Malone finishes the rainbow flag with a furious swipe of the purple crayon and sets the paper to one side. They pull out a clean sheet of white paper, select light pink and blue colors, and start coloring the trans flag. Noah figures this must be some kind of art-therapy for them.

"I feel so fucked up about it, you know? Everyone was working together for Agatha's school. All types of people. I was proud of us!" Malone says, echoing Noah's exact feeling from earlier. They shake their head, hastily finishing the last blue stripe. "But it just takes one hateful person to ruin everything, doesn't it?"

"Especially if they have a gun," Elena mumbles. She lets out a rush of air and makes a sign of the cross. "I just thank God he didn't hurt anyone."

Malone grabs a roll of tape out of the box and sticks a few pieces on the flags. Then they head to the door of the family bathroom.

"What are you doing?" Elena asks.

"Having some damn pride," Malone says, slapping the flags onto the door.

Noah does not like seeing them there. Lots of little alarm bells are ringing throughout his body, and he does not like the way the strangers passing by are hushed and staring. But now that the flags are up, it feels wrong to ask Malone to take them down.

"Take them down," Elena growls. Noah's stomach churns at the anger in her voice. He shares a nervous glance with David and Michael.

"No," Malone says. "I'm not going to live in fear because of a shit-stain like Roger Thibodeaux."

"You think Roger's the only shit-stain in this arena who hates f*****s," Elena says, standing up. She steps towards the door and grabs the corner of the trans flag, but Malone claps a hand over it, holding it in place.

"We have nothing to be ashamed of," Malone says. "Hiding who we are only plays into their prejudices."

"You think I'm hiding who I am?" Elena says, drawing up to her full height. "There are times for pride, and there are times to survive, and this here's a *survival* situation." Elena pulls the paper, ripping the trans flag down the line of Malone's hand. Malone's mouth falls open and their arm drops, their eyebrows knitting together in anger.

"Since we got here, I've caught that asshole Thibodeaux glaring at me too many times to count," Elena says, tearing down the rainbow flag, "and he's *not* the only one. I'm a trans woman of color — I've already got a target on my back. I don't need you hanging them on the walls to boot."

"I'm a trans *person* of color too," Malone mumbles rebelliously.

David sucks his teeth, and Michael cringes.

"Child, please. You think you know my struggle because you *changed yo pwonouns?* You have no fucking idea what I've sacrificed to be me. So don't act like you're some queer hero for this little ... craft project." Elena tosses the torn pieces of the flags at Malone's feet.

Malone looks like they want to say something but can't push out the words.

"Hey," David says, standing up. "Let's not fight like this ..."

"Shut up white man," Elena snaps. She turns back to Malone. "You know them good ol' boys love a hot Asian girl, and whatever you wanna call yourself, that's what you look like to them. But me?" She swipes a hand down the side of her body. "Ain't nothing they hate more than a Mexican tranny."

"Eh," someone says, "that's debatable." Agatha has returned, her eyes sweeping over the scene. "What's going on? Why are we playing oppression Olympics?"

Elena locks eyes with her, and the anger drains from her face, leaving only exhaustion and hurt. She drops to her cot, sitting among torn pieces of the trans flag. Agatha weaves through the cots to sit beside her friend.

Malone drops to Noah's cot, wiping tears off their face with a shirtsleeve. When they finally speak, their voice shakes with uncertainty. "You're right, okay? I shouldn't compare our struggles. But it's not true that I've never sacrificed anything." They take a deep, steadying breath. "My parents stopped paying my tuition when I introduced my girlfriend to them. I had to transfer to community college and start paying my way through school. I'm not saying that's as big of a deal as what you've been through, but it hasn't exactly been easy."

Noah clears his throat, which has felt bricked up since Elena and Malone started fighting. "I waited 'til graduation to come out to my parents," he says, "because I was scared they'd do the same thing. Maybe that makes me a coward —"

Malone snorts. "It's smart. I wish I'd done that."

"Well, I think you're brave," he tells them. "But I'm with Elena, about the flags. I don't want any extra attention while we're in here."

"I'm sorry," Malone whispers. "I should have asked y'all about it first."

Elena fiddles with the torn pieces of the trans flag. "I'm sorry too." She smiles sheepishly at Malone, then turns to Agatha. "Where's the podium?"

Agatha squints in confusion.

"For the ceremony? Because — we're clear on this, right? — I totally won the 'Oppression Olympics.'"

When the laughter dies down, Agatha sighs. "That man today was so awful. Let's not be awful to each other too."

The following day, the Red Cross posts a sign calling for volunteers, and Noah heads to the meetup, hoping to recapture that sense of purpose from the day before. He's given a locker to store his backpack, and without it his shoulders feel oddly naked. In the parking lot outside the arena, the volunteers learn how to set up massive tents for the refugees who are still pouring in from Houston and the wildfires out west. The Gulf may have been drenched by Hurricane Martha, but the rest of Texas has faced an endless summer of the worst drought in recorded history, and now much of it is burning.

After a few minutes working in the unnaturally hot September sun, Noah reluctantly sheds his hoodie. He curses himself for not getting his top surgery done while he had the chance. There are cops everywhere today — inside the arena and out — and Noah feels the hatred radiating from some of their eyes, as tangibly as the sun scorching the top of his head through his thick black hair. By mid-afternoon the temperature climbs to ninety degrees, and he soaks his clothes with sweat. Everyone is too hot to talk or joke around. When they finally head back into the AC, Noah does not feel good, as he'd hoped. He has that end-of-the-world feeling he'd gotten on the parking garage roof, watching the floodwaters tear his city apart.

At least he is so bone-tired that when he hits his cot, he falls instantly into a dreamless sleep. No time to wonder about his parents or roommates, ranked among the half-a-million missing. No visits from Abe to torment him. And for that reason alone, he goes back to volunteer the following day, and every day after, as the broad expanse of the parking lot fills with long, white tents. And every day, more people arrive to occupy them. The tents are hooked to AC units, but they're still eighty degrees inside in the middle of the day. Noah is grateful for his cot inside the arena. Especially one afternoon, when he passes the long, winding line for the outdoor canteen, and he notices a familiar shock of white hair.

Heart slamming in his chest, Noah rushes up to the nearest cop.

"Excuse me." He points his thumb over his shoulder at Roger Thibodeaux. "That guy there — that's the guy who pulled the gun in the arena!"

The cop slowly swings his gaze down to Noah. "So?" he asks.

"So —" Noah's words fail him as he looks at the cop. A stubble of blonde hair cut in a flat-top, a sneer reflected in his watery blue eyes.

"Roger Thibodeaux had a license for that gun. We put it in storage at the station, and he was discharged," the cop drawls.

"But he's violent!" Noah stammers. "He was yelling slurs and making threats!"

The cop shifts his weight and hooks his thumbs in his belt. He stares over the top of Noah's head. "You don't like him? He doesn't like you. So stay away from each other."

There is hatred in the cop's voice when he says *he doesn't like you.* Agreement.

And then color is draining away from the cop's uniform. The blue fades to black, the pink pigment drips out of his skin. Noah backs away, heart filling with dread. Abe has left him alone for nearly a week, and he'd hoped the visions were done. But now the badge on the cop's chest shrinks into an iron cross, and the patch on his arm bleeds into a red armband with a staring white eye — its pupil, a twisted black cross.

It's all in your head, Noah tells himself, forcing his feet to walk, not run, away from this figure from his nightmares. Everywhere now, color is dripping out of the world, and the white rows of tents against a grey sky remind him of a far more sinister camp. Down the next aisle, he spots another cop-turned-SS guard in black and white and that horrible slash of red. He rounds the corner of a tent to avoid him and finds himself face-to-chest with a tall man in a Nazi uniform. He bolts. Voices shout, barking German orders. He hurtles through the labyrinth of tents, taking turns at random, heading in the general direction of the arena, praying that the visions will quit once he's inside.

Then he trips — flies through the air and smacks the ground hard. His chest hits first, knocking the breath from his lungs, then his palms and forehead crack into the pavement.

A weight smashes into his back, so he can't suck in new air. Hands slap his body up and down — thighs, legs, chest. What do they want with him? And is any of this real, or is it all part of Abe's vision?

"*It's* not carrying anything," says the man kneeling on Noah's back. The pronoun drips with loathing.

"Pulaski, that's *enough*. Sir — sir? Are you alright?" comes a kinder voice.

The weight lifts, and he sucks in a lungful of air. Someone helps him to a seat. A thick length of electrical cord is wrapped around his ankle. He touches his forehead, and his fingertips come away wet — and Nazi armband red.

"Why were you running away from our officers?" This cop is wearing the uniform of the Dallas Police Department. The flat-top cop, the one who'd been kneeling on his back, is dressed in navy too.

"I'm sorry, I saw —" Noah is so disoriented that he almost tells the truth — then pulls up short. Cops are not the people to confide in about mental health issues. "I saw that guy who had the AR-15, and I just ... freaked. I'm sorry."

The nice cop asks where his tent is, and he explains that he's actually a volunteer from inside the arena. She offers to escort him there and helps him to his feet. She's a white woman with a short haircut, who forces her voice a little deeper than its natural range, and Noah would bet his binder that she's some kind of queer.

At the arena doors, she gives his upper arm a squeeze. "You let me know if anyone gives you a hard time. Ask for Sergeant Levin."

He thanks her, then heads inside, shaky with adrenaline. He feels sick about thanking her. He feels sick thinking how much worse that could've gone, if his skin hadn't been white, if Sergeant Levin hadn't stepped in. But most of all, he feels sick with dread about what's happening inside his own mind.

This vision lasted much longer than any of the others, and he hadn't just seen Nazis, he'd *believed* they were real. He'd forgotten it was a vision and panicked. He'd lost control.

Despite a life-long skepticism, a growing part of Noah's mind believes that Abe is real. And this time, the ghost hadn't saved his life — it had almost gotten him killed.

Depart, Depart!

On Friday morning, David catches Noah in the lunch line. "Hey, you're Jewish, right?" the older man asks.

"Sort of? Culturally, I guess?" Noah answers. "But we weren't religious. I never had a Bat Mitzvah or anything."

"There's a group of us here from my temple — very Reform, very progressive — we're getting together for Shabbos tonight, up in the school rooms. Do you want to come with me?"

"To be honest, I don't really believe —"

David waves his hand like it's nothing. "Plenty of Jews don't believe. But there's value in tra-di-tion, right?" He says it like Tevye from *Fiddler on the Roof*, rearing back and making two fists. "It'll be great — getting together with other Jews, with your mishpocheh!"

The Yiddish tugs on something in Noah's heart. David's mannerisms remind him of his dad in a way that both aches and soothes him. Maybe he's supposed to do this — find out more about Judaism — maybe it's the key to freeing himself from Abe.

Before sundown, Noah and David head upstairs to the school rooms. In the largest suite overlooking the court, a dozen people stand around a middle-aged woman who waves her hands over two candles and recites a prayer in Hebrew.

An unfolded paper napkin covers her hair as she speak-sings the mysterious syllables. Noah is suddenly dizzy with the memory of his grandmother, Yetta — Herschel's wife. Yetta always lit the candles on Friday nights, despite the scoffing of the men in the family, all atheists. Noah had always longed to be invited into that secret ceremony. He was sure there was magic in the ritual, but never let his interest show, for fear of his father's scathing derision of anything supernatural.

Suddenly Noah remembers a third story about Abe. It's from way back in his memory, before grandpa Herschel got diagnosed with stomach cancer, so Noah must have been five or six years old. Herschel sat at their dinner table after a meal, describing how his father, Abe, had taught him Hebrew with a ruler in one hand and a matchstick in the other.

"He would give me a passage to read and point to each letter with the matchstick. If I made one tiny little mistake, whack!" Herschel slammed his huge hand on the table next to Noah's tiny one, making him jump. "Down came the ruler. My knuckles bled by the end of every lesson." He rubbed his hands as if they still ached after all this time. "I didn't know what any of the words meant, mind you, but I learned to read Hebrew perfectly. God forbid I embarrass my father at temple. Abe was a very respected man in the synagogue, you know? Of course, this was before he ran out on the family, the schmuck."

Noah can't believe he'd forgotten this — the origin of his family's patrilineal atheism. Maybe it's because the stories about Abe don't add up. He can't square this image-obsessed Abe with the drifter from dad's cigar shop or with the boy in the duffel bag who keeps haunting his waking hours.

There's nowhere to wash their hands, so the congregants pass around a bottle of hand sanitizer, everyone chuckling when it's their turn for a pump. David hands out paper cups of wine, and Noah is surprised to find it's real. Alcohol is banned inside the shelter, so he hasn't had a drop since the tequila, that night Martha made landfall. The woman who reminds him so much of his grandmother blesses a loaf of challah.

Noah doesn't think of Yetta often, but now his heart surges with a complicated grief. Yetta used to say things like, "In my day, girls wore shoes to make our feet look as tiny as possible," shaking her head at Noah's chunky boots. "Girls your age should paint their nails." "Girls in my day didn't go to the barbershop." Even still, he knew Yetta had loved him. Whenever he visited the assisted living facility where Yetta spent her last years, his grandmother would beam, and show him off to friends, and pat his hand, saying what a good heart he had. Maybe, since Yetta had spotted Noah's failure at femininity from the start, she would have understood when he told her he was really a man. Yetta died before he came out, so he'll never know, but he wonders if there's any harm in pretending.

After the blessings, everyone gets in line to fix a plate, and the woman who reminds him of Yetta comes over and introduces herself as Sadie.

"Noah," Sadie says. "David told us about you. I'm so glad you decided to come."

"Thanks," Noah says. "It's been nice."

"We're very progressive, you know. Most progressive temple in Houston. We're LBGT allies," she says, holding up a fist.

Noah smiles. She's trying.

"You know when I was a girl, I was *also* quite the tomboy."

Noah's smile falls. David tries to interrupt, but Sadie cuts him off.

"So I understand your kind better than most. But I do have to wonder about — Well, you know how Jews aren't supposed to get tattoos? It's in Leviticus."

"Come on, Sadie, there's a lot of bullshit in Leviticus that we ignore," David says. "We're Reform! We also trim our beards and wear mixed fabrics."

"I'm just saying, every human body is a beautiful gift from God. So be whatever gender you want! But when it comes to taking these hormones and getting these surgeries, I ... I wonder why people can't love the body God gave them?"

Noah is stunned and hurting, like he'd bent to smell a rose and gotten stung by a wasp. "Excuse me," he mumbles, handing David his plate. "I'm not hungry anymore."

He hurries out of the suite, reeking of food that suddenly nauseates. Emerging into the hallway, he freezes in horror. All down the corridor, graffiti covers the walls from floor to ceiling: *Jude. Juden. Juden Raus!* Swastikas and Stars of David punctuate the words in still-dripping black paint.

David bursts into the hall. "Noah — I'm so sorry." He doesn't react to the writing on the walls, so Noah knows it's all

41

in his head. Another torment from Abe. But why — why show him this? The ghost boy isn't around to ask.

"Why did you bring me here?" Noah demands, rounding on David instead. If he hadn't come, he wouldn't have got to thinking about Yetta, and caring what Sadie thought, and he wouldn't have seen this scene out of Kristallnacht that isn't even fucking real. "Do you agree with her? Do you think I'm *desecrating the temple of my body* by transitioning?"

"Of course not!" David says. "I didn't know Sadie would say any of that stuff — and I gave her a piece of my mind, for what it's worth."

"You think the human body is perfect? Tell that to your fucking appendix. Tell that to all the women — I mean — *people* with uteruses who die in childbirth. Tell that to folks with ALS or kids who get cancer or fucking ... There's no plan to this shit, no design." He smacks his bound chest. "It's all random organs and DNA that *happened* to make it through natural selection, okay? Why the fuck shouldn't I cut my tits off if I don't want them?"

Noah is shouting at David, who he knows doesn't deserve it, but he can't seem to stop himself.

"Noah, I support your transition," David says. "I'm so sorry Sadie said that stuff to you."

"It's hard enough being trans here. Why are you making me be Jewish too? How many things have I got to be hated for?"

"I'm not making you be Jewish, Noah. You *are* Jewish."

"You know what I never got," Noah waves a hand at the graffiti-scarred walls, even though he knows that all David sees is a broad expanse of white. "Why the fuck didn't my ancestors just *quit*? A thousand years of wandering around Europe — blend the fuck in, people! All the pogroms and shit, for what? Some hocus-pocus about lighting candles?"

Now it's David who looks furious. His voice shakes with the effort of control. "I would think that you, of all people, would understand that there are parts of your identity worth fighting for. Even — no, *especially* in the face of persecution."

Noah catches David's meaning and his stomach roils with shame. David heads down the stairwell in disgust. Noah's eyes well with tears, and when they spill, the walls are stark-white again, no trace of the desecration. His mind feels cleaned-up too, scrubbed of anger.

"I'm sorry." Noah chases after David. "I shouldn't have said that."

"Ach." David makes a distinctly Yiddish sound. He flicks his hand at the wrist — a gesture his dad uses to mean, "I'm done with you." It stops Noah in his tracks. He watches David dwindle down the stairs, feeling like his heart is cracking open, coming to a sudden understanding.

"Maybe ... maybe it's that I'm jealous," Noah calls. David slows. "I don't have your faith ... or any kind of promise that there's a point to all this shit. The truth is I'm really *not* Jewish, and I'll never be, because everyone who could've taught me what that means is gone." Noah chokes on the last word, and then he has to sit on the stairs, because he can't see for the tears filling his eyes. After a while, he feels David's arm on his back, and he leans towards the man's shoulder.

"Now what are you talking about, you don't know how to be Jewish?" David says, in the sing-song cadence Herschel always used to preface a joke. "You've got the self-hating part down pat!"

Noah coughs a laugh and stares down at his lap. "The worst part is, like, the shit Sadie was saying? Sometimes it's in my head too."

David doesn't respond, waiting for Noah to go on.

"I say I haven't gotten top surgery, because I don't have the money. And that's true. But also ... I haven't tried to save it. I never made a crowdfunding site or anything. It's not that I don't want it." Noah can't believe he's saying this stuff out loud for the first time. "When I imagine what it would be like to have a flat chest — it's incredible. I'd be so free. I *don't doubt that.*" He punctuates each word with a slash of his hand. "But when I imagine the surgery itself? The cutting?"

"Any kind of surgery is scary," David offers.

"Yeah, but plenty of trans guys do it, they can't *wait* to do it. But there's this voice in my head saying, '*Those surgeries are for Gentiles! Your ancestors didn't die in the pogroms for you to cut off perfectly good body parts!*'" He's imitating his dad's voice, and it makes David laugh.

"And my grandpa — he hated hospitals. My grandma had to fight to get him to every chemo treatment. He'd say they were poisoning him, which — well, they were. He'd say, '*You know what the Nazis did to the Jews in* their *hospitals?*'" Noah smiles bitterly. "He was terrible to the nurses."

"I can imagine," David nods, chuckling. "You know that — whether you get the surgery or not — it doesn't make you any less of a man."

"Yeah, I know," Noah says, but his throat is tight, because hearing it from David makes it easier to believe. "But there's a lot of people who don't think that way."

"You know, this kind of LGBT-friendly Temple — imperfect as it is — nothing remotely like this existed when I was growing up," David says. "It was not easy being a gay Jewish boy in the 1960's. In *Texas* — are you kidding?" He coughs a bitter laugh. "All my life, I've had to fight to be seen as a 'real man,' a 'real Jew.' So ... I know a bit about what that's like."

David's voice is so kind that Noah finally gathers the courage to ask what's been tugging at the back of his mind all night.

"Can I ask you something random?" David nods and Noah takes a breath before continuing. "Do Jews believe in ghosts?"

"Sure," David spreads his hands wide. "When I was a kid, if I was being wild, my bubbe would say I had a 'dybbuk on my back.'"

"A dybbuk?" Noah repeats.

"It's like, the ghost of an evil person who possesses you." David waggles his fingers eerily. "Of course, I'm sure it was all

44

just a way to explain mental illness, neurodiversity — that sort of thing. I got diagnosed with ADHD a few years ago — in my sixties, if you can believe it! But to my bubbe, I was 'possessed by a dybbuk!'"

"Right," Noah says. Because ghosts aren't real — even religious people know that.

"Why? Have you seen a ghost in the arena?" David teases in a spooky voice.

"Oh, no," Noah blushes and looks back up the stairs, checking that the walls behind are still white. "Just feeling a little haunted lately ... by everything."

"Oh, right. Of course," David says. And for a while they sit together in silence, both thinking of the people they have most likely lost.

🕊

Life in the shelter falls into a rhythm. Noah volunteers with the Red Cross every day, sometimes sorting donations, sometimes setting up tents in the heat. Sometimes he sees Roger Thibodeaux, who, in a concerning development, has made friends. He's always hanging with a group of angry-looking rednecks, most of whom look like they could snap Noah into pieces without breaking a sweat. Now, Noah always heads to and from his work site in a group. If he has to piss, but no one else does, he holds it rather than risk the port-a-potties alone.

In the evenings at Montrose Dos, they play cards, watch movies on Noah's laptop, or trade dog-eared paperbacks. They complain about the food, which gets steadily worse. One night, dinner is a scoop of rice with a slice of American cheese, and Malone corners one of the Red Cross coordinators, demanding an explanation. He tells them that with Texas's biggest port underwater and half its farmland on fire, grocery stores all over Dallas are running out of food. Hearing that makes all the hairs on Noah's arms stand up.

At the end of their second week in the shelter, two of the cots in Montrose Dos are empty at lights-out.

"Where are David and Michael?" Noah asks Elena.

"They left this afternoon," she says, without looking up from her book. "David looked for you at lunch. He wanted to say goodbye."

"I — I ate outside. Where did they go?"

"A hotel room, probably? Their bank was underwater for a while — *literally* — but they got access to their money again today, and — yeah they split."

Noah drops to his cot, feeling gutted. Since that last Shabbos, he's felt closer to David than anyone in the arena. "Did David leave a number? Or an email address? Shit, I don't even know his last name!"

"Nope, and I bet that's on purpose. They don't want us hitting them up for help."

"No ... I can't believe that," Noah shakes his head.

"That's what people with money do. Everyone who can afford to is getting out of here as fast as they can. Haven't you noticed?"

Now that she's mentioned it, there are faces he's come to recognize that have vanished, and new ones he's never seen before. "I guess I didn't think about it. I didn't really know we were *allowed* to leave."

Elena snickers. "Of course you can leave, but where you gonna go if you don't have any money? No connections in Dallas? Nah, I've been homeless before. This shelter isn't bad as far as they go. I'll take a roof over my head and three square meals until they kick us out."

"Or until the food runs out ..." Noah trails off, thinking of what the Red Cross worker had said. He rounds on Elena. "Do you promise you're not gonna leave too?"

"Poor folk have no choice but to stick together. But what about you, white boy? You sitting on a trust fund over there? Holding out on us?"

Noah shakes his head. "I have $47 in my account."

"Ooooh, better not go shouting about it," Elena laughs. "Folks'll start hitting you up for those big bucks!"

After that conversation, Noah pays attention to the changes in the arena, the flux of people coming and going. Some of the new folks are refugees from the burning of Austin. They're always coughing, all night long, like they've still got ash in their lungs. A group of orphaned children arrive, so Agatha's school becomes a 24-hour orphanage, and she rarely visits the promenade anymore. Malone's college friends leave one by one, as they get in touch with relatives, and the butch couple with the cat disappear, and then it's just Malone, Elena, and Noah left from the original Montrose Dos.

In that first mad dash into the arena, most people had grabbed the first free cots they saw, so everyone was all mixed up. But as new folks trickle in, they tend to set down their stuff near people who look like home, just as Noah did that first night when he spotted Elena. In this way, the arena gradually becomes almost as visibly divided along racial and ethnic lines as the old neighborhoods of Houston. Noah is one of the only white people who doesn't live on the central court, where the lights are brightest, where there's always a few cops keeping watch.

Of course there are exceptions — pockets of diversity. Montrose Dos is one. Another is the group of people who have taken to sleeping through the day in the third-tier arena chairs, their heads at funny angles. Noah doesn't give them much thought until his volunteer group is assigned to clean up the bleachers one day, and all down the rows of seats he finds empty bottles of alcohol, plastic baggies, cooked spoons, and syringes. Soon after, he notices how the stairwells have started to reek of beer and cigarettes, weed and piss.

The tent city now sprawls across three city blocks of Dallas. At night, the western sky glows orange, where wildfires are devouring the far suburbs. The air is filled with smoke, and the paper masks the Red Cross volunteers are given to wear don't help much. Noah coughs all night after a day working outside. He's increasingly grateful to be assigned indoors, cleaning the air-conditioned arena. No matter how they try, though, they can't keep up with the mess. Graffiti spreads like a mold over the walls and stalls and arena seats — Houston sports team logos and the names of drowned neighborhoods appear faster than they can clean or paint them over. Spiders colonize the rafters of the building, and the corners become caked with grime — the accumulated sloughed skin cells of two thousand humans who never leave.

Probably in response to the deteriorating hygiene, drug use, and rumors of sexual assault, the Red Cross decides the arena should become an adults-only shelter. Agatha is to leave with her orphans and the last of the families. She stops by the cots to say goodbye and gives Elena a long hug. Damien and Kayla are going with her, and Damien gives Noah a pound on the back. They never became friends or anything, but always acknowledged each other in passing, and Noah will miss even that small kindness.

With the exodus of the children, it's much quieter in the arena. No more babies crying or kids laughing and fighting with siblings. Noah sticks to Montrose Dos when he isn't working, feeling uneasy everywhere else. Remembering David's story about his bubbe, he's started researching dybbuks on his laptop, often reading by the glow of his screen late into the night, after everyone else has fallen asleep.

He learns that a belief in ghosts is as common a feature of human society as music or dancing or gods. Nearly every culture on earth has some tradition of spirit possession, a fact that sends chills down his spine. But he reminds himself this ubiquity doesn't necessarily mean there's truth to the stories — just that it's fundamentally human to want the dead to linger.

For Jews, the first mention of spirit possession appears in the book of Samuel. When King Saul was possessed by an evil spirit, a young David knew how to cure him. "And it came to pass, when the ELOHIM spirit was upon Saul, that David took the harp, and played with his hand; so Saul found relief ... and the evil spirit departed from him." Noah understands this story intimately — how a certain tune, played on repeat, can bring one relief and chase evil spirits away. When he was a teenager, didn't certain songs by the Mountain Goats and Sleater-Kinney do as much for him?

He learns that after that first musical, bibilical exorcism, spirit possession was pretty rare in Jewish communities until an explosion of cases in the mid-sixteenth century. The whole of Europe and the Middle East was a bit obsessed with the occult around that time. Christians were burning witches across Europe, and the Spanish Inquisition drove hundreds of thousands of Jews from the Iberian peninsula. Many of the exiled Jews resettled in Israel, in the city of Safed, where the ghosts were notoriously restless.

Maybe it was this displacement that made the Jews of Safed so receptive to the Kabbala's doctrine of *gilgul ha neshamot* — the cycling of souls. As they fled the Inquisition, the Iberian exiles could not take the bones of their ancestors with them, but they could take comfort in the belief that the spirits of their elders returned to live among them. Particularly holy spirits might be reborn as infants, emerging as spiritual leaders later in life. Devout men even induced spirit possession in themselves, calling down the ghosts of their ancestors to inhabit their bodies and share wisdom in times of crisis. But ghosts were not always a blessing. If the soul of a sinner was too impure to enter Gehinnom, it would be cast back into the mortal world as punishment. And when one of these wandering souls found their way into the body of a living person, they were called "dybbuk."

That night, he gets so excited that he shares what he's reading with Elena and Malone out loud, without even thinking. "Hey so you know how Catholics think people get possessed by demons, and Muslims think people get possessed by djinns? And those are both, like, supernatural *beings*, right? Non-human. But dybbuks — that's Jewish ghosts — they're just like, real people. Sinners. Some relative or neighbor who fucked over their village."

He's broken out in a cold sweat. All the pieces added up — Wasn't great-grandfather Abe a sinner? Didn't he run out on his family, when Herschel was only fourteen years old, leaving them to grapple with his debts?

"Okay ..." Malone says, drawing out the word.

"Dybbuks have to come back to the world of the living as punishment. But it's also, like, a chance for redemption? I think?" Noah says.

"That's very interesting Noah," Elena says, in a Kindergarten-teacher voice, "But why, exactly, are we learning about Jewish ghosts?"

Noah falters. "Oh — I, uh, you know. Googling random stuff."

The others nod, and Noah keeps his research to himself after that. He doesn't want his friends finding out that the reason he's obsessed with dybbuks is that he keeps seeing a boy who isn't there.

He dives into feminist scholarship on dybbuks, putting himself in the shoes of someone unfortunate enough to be assigned female at birth in a medieval Jewish village. Many girls were married off at twelve or thirteen, to men often twice their age! Child brides faced the terrifying prospect of childbirth while they, themselves, were still children. Wives worked tirelessly as servants to their husbands, expected to "submit to their own husbands, as to the lord" in every little thing — or else, as the philosopher Maimonides instructed, they should be "compelled to do so, even with the rod." And so domestic violence and marital rape wasn't just tolerated, but divinely ordained.

But if a dybbuk got ahold of you, well — you were impure, tainted by the dead, and a Jewish man wouldn't touch you. Was it any wonder, then, that the historical records of possession were mostly of young women — newly engaged or brides? Not only were possessed women freed from their husband's hands, but suddenly they had a voice that was listened to — the voice of a dead *man*. And several of these women managed to swing this in their favor, establishing careers as mystics and prophets-for-hire.

When he imagines himself as a medieval AFAB person, forced to marry some cis dude his parents picked out, forced to be a good little wifey for the rest of his days, Noah decides spirit possession sounds highly preferable — even though a disconcerting number of the possessed died. Maybe it was because the patients succumbed to whatever underlying medical condition was being taken for spirit possession. Or maybe it was because the methodology of exorcism could be deadly. A crowd of old men would gather around you, chanting day and night, pouring potions down your throat that might be poison. Several of the victims were reported "strangled" by their dybbuks, and scholars wonder if they didn't asphyxiate from all the perfumed smoke used to treat them.

One night, he reads that the famous exorcist Rabbi Vital believed his own wife Hannah was born with a male soul, and Noah feels like all his blood has gone electric. Is this evidence of trans acknowledgment —even *acceptance* —among medieval Jews? He reads on, discovering that Kabbalists believed infertility and homosexuality could be caused by a male soul reincarnating in a woman's body. Would his brand of gender nonconformity have been understood this way as well?

Noah tumbles down a rabbit hole of googling *gilgul*, and he forgets all about Abe and dybbuks and the visions that have haunted him. He's discovered a Jewish spiritual framework for transness, dating back five hundred years, and he feels robbed that he'd never heard of it. Why hasn't anyone told him that Hebrew has pronouns for six genders, acknowledging a spectrum of intersex people? Why hadn't he known the lines, *"God created Adam in His image, in the image of God He created him; male and female God created them"* were interpreted by Jewish sages to mean that Adam was initially androgynous — *both* male and female? Why had no one told him that from ancient times, Jews have understood that gender and sex are spectrums, distinct from one another, and that this is his tradition too, if he chooses to claim it!

He knows the answer, of course. It's the same reason that he's ignorant about all Jewish religious thought — because he comes from a family of atheists, because of Abe with the matchstick and the ruler, beating the Hebrew syllables and an indelible hatred of religion into Herschel. When Noah remembers this, he comes crashing back to his body, stretched on the hard, nylon cot. He's been grasping at straws, clinging to scraps of a religion he doesn't believe in, quotes by rabbis who believed women were less than people, who would've sold Noah, when he was still a prepubescent child, into marital slavery. Why should he look to such men for any kind of validation or guidance?

Besides, the stories of dybbuks don't even fit what's happening to Noah. They don't tell of the possessed seeing *visions* of the dead, but of having their bodies taken over — falling down in epileptic fits, speaking prophecies in voices that were not their own. And sure, he fainted that one time at Agatha's school, but that was probably dehydration. And sure, it was a bit prophetic how he knew the flood was coming, but that was just his intuition. Abe has never taken hold of his body, as if he were a puppet. And Noah has never exhibited xenoglossia — speaking in languages unknown to him — which is widely cited as the only "certain" evidence of possession.

Still, he reads on, late into each night, long after everyone around him is snoring. Finally, when the characters on the screen begin to blur, he closes his laptop, slips it into his bag, and curls around it. Fragments of history and scripture drift through his mind. He tells himself they're all nonsense. He clings to them like lifelines.

Noah gets back late from volunteering one evening, so Malone and Elena are already at the dinner line. Sticky with sweat, he decides to take another paper-towel bath. Locked in the bathroom, he is scrubbing between his legs, when he notices a splotch of dark red on the paper towels.

His ears ring as he stares at the blood. All week he's felt sluggish and achy — like he was fighting off a cold. But now he understands. He drops naked onto the toilet. What was it David had said? "It doesn't make you any less of a man." But with his uterus starting to cramp, and his breasts lying flat on his stomach, he can't quite believe it, can't shake the feeling that the past year of his life, he's been struggling in vain for something impossible. He fights back tears, slowly winding up toilet paper into a makeshift maxi-pad.

Then — *SLAM!* The door reverberates, like someone has hurled their whole body into it. Noah's heart pounds in his ears. He desperately wants to pull on some clothes, but he is frozen with fear on the cold toilet. The door handle rattles. It's locked. Outside, men are laughing, and there's a long, hissing sound.

Noah's body refuses to move until it's been silent for many long minutes. He pulls on clothes with shaking arms and crosses to the door. Was that real? Or is Abe messing with him again? A ghost or a hallucination? And does it even matter, when his fear is so real?

If someone is waiting outside, he doesn't want them trapping him in the small room. In one motion, he twists the bolt-lock and slams open the door, bursting into the promenade.

The few people around stare past his shoulder. One woman holds a hand over her mouth. He turns.

On the door of the bathroom, in still-dripping spray paint, someone has written the slur F*****S. He touches the paint, which comes away on his finger. Armband red. Real.

"Who did this?" he demands of the people standing around, but they shake their heads, hold up their hands, and hurry off. "Who did this!" he roars. No one answers, and his voice echoes down the promenade, too shrill, the voice of someone small and terrified.

He scrubs at the paint, but the paper towels only smear the slur at the edges. He finds a Red Cross worker, and they say they'll send someone by to clean it up. Malone and Elena return, their Styrofoam trays laden with creamed corn and canned pineapple. Malone cries when they see the word on the door, and Elena gets very quiet. Someone from the Red Cross finally shows up with a can of white paint to slather over the slur. The white doesn't match the original grey of the door, and when it dries, the letters still bleed through in pale pink.

The next day, Noah doesn't go to his volunteer meetup as usual, spending the morning on his laptop instead. He wants to do something for Elena and Malone, make them feel safe again. For some reason, the thought of saving *them* feels a lot less overwhelming than the thought of saving himself.

His first thought is that he needs a job. Get money, so he can get them out of there. But as he's searching for "trans-inclusive workplaces" he comes across The Rainbow House, the kind of catch-all place that has queer AA meetings, STD testing, and homeless services for LGBT youth. He gives them a call.

Later, he tracks down Elena and Malone watching TV in one of Agatha's old classrooms. The reporter on-screen is walking through a grocery store, showing aisle after aisle of empty shelves.

"Get your stuff," Noah grins. "We're taking a trip."

They take an Uber to The Rainbow House, a three-story office building that looks decidedly beige on the outside, and spend a few hours shuttling to various offices. A doctor writes Elena and Noah scripts for hormones, and Noah clutches the scrap of paper like it's a million-dollar check.

But his highest hopes are dashed when they meet with the housing coordinator. "I'm so sorry," says Bethany, a femme blonde with a north Texas accent. "But we're having to refer all you out-of-towners to the Red Cross shelters. We really only have the resources to focus on homeless youth *from* the Dallas-Fort Worth area."

"You can't send us back to that shelter," Elena says. She tells the woman about the slur on the bathroom door.

"That sounds awful. I'm so sorry that happened to you," Bethany drawls. She crinkles her eyebrows at them in sympathy. "Can I call you an Uber?"

"Why can't we stay here?" Malone pleads. "There's got to be a couch or something! What if we refuse to leave?"

"I'm afraid that wouldn't be very safe," Bethany says. "And we try not to involve the police."

The threat registers. Elena stands, and they follow her out the door.

Noah's phone navigates them to a pharmacy where they get their prescriptions filled. In the bathroom, Noah gives himself a shot, and by the time he meets Elena and Malone outside, he already feels a surge of energy. The sun is setting over the Dallas skyline, burning-suburbia-orange. He can't bear to go back to the arena. "This must be the queer neighborhood right? Let's get a drink. I can afford a round of Lone Stars."

"Better yet," Malone grins. "I'll find someone else to buy us drinks."

Malone pays for another car share to a lesbian bar called The Pink Slipper. It's two-two-Tuesdays, where all drinks are two dollars, and all the music is from the 2000's. Blu Cantrell blares as they muscle inside, and Elena cries, "Ooooh, this is my jam," and heads for the dance floor.

Noah follows Malone to the bar, and within moments, a handsome butch named Carla, with grey at her temples, offers to buy them both a drink. Carla has a rasping drawl and asks Malone what part of town they're from. When she hears they're from Houston, Carla drags over a bar stool. She grills them with questions about the hurricane, and Noah grows quiet. He thought they were coming here to forget everything for a while, not put their tragedy on display to impress some biker chick.

Noah brings a second beer to Elena on the dance floor, but she waves it away, shouting over the music that she's sober. So, double-fisting, he tries dancing to Lady Gaga, but his limbs won't cooperate. When "Poker Face" came out, Noah was eleven years old, and now he can't figure out how to dance to the song in a way that doesn't make him feel like an eleven-year-old girl. There's a few other men dancing, and he watches them to imitate their moves, but they're gay guys, moving in a feminine way. He catches himself in these thoughts and feels guilty — what's wrong with "dancing like a girl" anyways? Is he such a misogynist? Is his masculinity so fragile?

He pounds both beers, dumps the empty bottles in the trash, and returns to Elena with a swimming head. He drops to a low squat, twists his ass, and snakes his chest up towards her.

"Yassss!" Elena cries, clapping her hands and grinning. "That's my boy!"

Noah loses his ego in the rhythm, moving in ways both handsome and elegant, not caring which is which. He recalls that ancient exorcism, when King David chased off an evil spirit with nothing more than his lyre. There's an undeniable magic in music. "Crazy in Love" comes on then, and Noah's dancing becomes a kind-of prayer to Beyoncé, patron saint of Houston, Texas. Dear Queen Bey, let me be cleansed. If I dance long and hard enough, let me shake this dybbuk off my back.

Many songs later, when his skin is slick with sweat and his throat scratches for a drink, he finally heads back to the bar. Malone is talking about daily life in the shelter, while Carla watches the movements of their perfectly arched lips. When Malone tells Carla what happened to Noah in the family bathroom, she cries, "No! They didn't write that!" and actually *looks* at Noah for the first time all night. He twists his mouth and nods awkwardly, wishing Malone hadn't dragged him into this. "I'm so sorry," Carla shakes her head. "I'm not gonna be able to sleep thinking of the two of you stuck in that place."

Malone smiles wryly. "We went to Rainbow House today, hoping they could hook us up with housing, or a better shelter. But they only care about Dallas queers, apparently."

Carla stares at them both for a few, long moments, then says, "Y'all should come with me. It's a small house, but I've got a spare bedroom and a finished basement. You'd have your own bathroom. You can stay until you get on your feet."

Malone looks at Noah, eyes sparking with excitement. The thought of a real house — far from Roger Thibodeaux, and sneering cops, with a real shower that doesn't run on a five-second timer — it's so beautiful Noah can hardly breathe.

And then he notices the figure perched on the bar stool beside Carla, a child, in black-and-white tintype. Noah's heart sinks to his stomach. So much for musical exorcisms. Abe is nodding at Carla — he wants Noah to accept her hospitality. But for the first time, Noah doubts Abe's judgment. There's something about Carla he doesn't like, and it's clear why she wants to get Malone in her house.

"Are you sure?" he asks Malone, casting a side-eye at Carla.

Malone purses their lips and nods, in a way he takes to mean, *I can handle her.*

"Let's ask Elena, then."

Carla frowns. "I'm sorry. Who's Elena?"

"She's our friend. She's right ..." Malone searches the dance floor and points to Elena, waving her hand to the beat of "Single Ladies."

Carla's smile tightens, than vanishes. "You know, I thought it was just the two of you. Like I said, it's a small house. I'm not sure there's room —"

"You said you had a spare bedroom *and* a finished basement," Malone says. "Trust me, we've been sleeping on cots for a month. It'll be plenty of space."

"But I forgot I've got friends coming into town this month, and work's gonna be crazy ..."

"We just need a place to sleep until we can get jobs," Malone says, amping up the flirtatious lilt in their voice. "We won't be any trouble."

"I'm afraid I only have space for the two of you," Carla says with finality.

Abe's ghost points frantically at Carla. Noah has never defied Abe's warnings before, and he's terrified of what will happen if he does. But now the boy wants him to abandon Elena to save himself. Is he capable of that? Slipping out of the club without a word to the woman who's become like a mother to him this long, horrible month? Is he supposed to leave her behind, as Abe left his family behind when he climbed into that duffel bag? Maybe this is what Abe is here to teach him — that the Jews who survived were the ones willing to abandon everything, and everyone.

Malone's shout startles him back to the present. "Bullshit, *you don't have room*. Bullshit! This is something about Elena, isn't it? What, she's not fuckable enough for you? 'Cause she's actually your age? Or is this a racist thing?"

Part of Noah wants to cheer, part of him is mourning the imagined shower, and part of him writhes with self-loathing for even considering ditching Elena.

"Seriously?" Carla sneers. "You're calling me racist? After I invited *you*?"

"Uch!" Malone gagged. "Okay Boomer, if you think yellow fever insulates you from racism then your head is even farther up your ass than I thought."

Carla stands, puffing her chest out. "Are you calling me a racist?"

Abe's ghost shakes his head regretfully, then vanishes.

Noah takes Malone's arm and pulls her towards the door. "Let's just go."

"What kind of man won't fight for their lady's honor?" Carla sneers at him.

"A Jewish one," he answers. "And they're not a lady."

Malone laughs, a little too hard, and lets Noah lead them away. He regrets the joke now. It's too much like something his dad would've said.

"We have to go," he tells Elena as they pass her, swaying to "Hold Up."

"What happened?" she asks outside.

Malone and Noah exchange a look, confirming that they won't tell Elena the whole story. "I — I had too many drinks and talked politics with some old white lady," Malone says.

Elena sighs and rolls her eyes. "Next time, can you wait till they're done playing Beyoncé?"

They get back to the arena past midnight. The wildfires are burning near the city limits now, and the tent city glows eerily in the orange, hazy twilight. They huddle together, walking briskly through the white-walled labyrinth. When they reach the arena, the doors are locked.

"You've got to be kidding me." Malone tugs at the long door handles.

"What are we going to do?" Noah asks.

Malone pounds on the glass and waves, as if they see someone inside.

A voice from behind startles them. "Step away from the door." Noah turns to find Officer Pulaski with his hands resting on his belt. Dread thickens in Noah's stomach.

"You wanna tell me why you're breaking and entering?"

"We live inside," Malone says. "Our cots are there, our stuff is there."

"Anybody could say that." Pulaski steps closer, and the three of them shrink back into the shadowed entryway. Noah's guts turn to water as the color starts to melt from the cop's uniform, the blue deepening to black. Pulaski pulls his nightstick from his belt.

Malone reiterates that they live inside, their voice now smaller, frightened. Elena stares at the ground. Noah casts his eyes around — and spots an unnaturally pale boy standing behind Pulaski.

"Help," Noah mouths silently.

The boy rushes forward without moving his legs, his skin blurring to grey, pausing only a moment to hover before his great-grandson's face, before passing inside Noah's skin.

Ice in his blood. Noah's body goes rigid, all his muscles freezing over. Pulaski's shoulder radio crackles with jargon, and the cop leans his head close to answer. At the moment Pulaski pushes the button on the side of the radio, Noah's vision goes black. He feels his mouth open, feels words ripped from his lungs, but they are not his own. He's falling. There's a crack of pain as his hip, and then the back of his skull, smack into something hard. He can't cry out — someone else is using his tongue.

And then his body lies still. He blinks his eyes open, rolls up to sit under his own power. Pulaski, Elena, and Malone all stare down at him, wearing similar expressions of shock.

A familiar voice crackles from Pulaski's shoulder radio. "This is Sergeant Levin. What the hell was that?"

Pulaski frowns and pushes the button to answer. "Just some crazy kid —"

"Sergeant Levin ..." Noah repeats, as the name registers — that butch cop, who'd saved him once before. "Sergeant Levin! We're at the North doors!" Pulaski's thumb pops off the transmitter, and Noah isn't sure if his words got through.

"I'm on my way," comes Levin's voice. "Pulaski, stay put until I get there."

Noah puts a hand to the back of his throbbing skull, relieved to find it's not broken. "What happened?"

"You had a seizure or something. And you were shouting — I think it was German?" Elena says.

"I don't know, I took German, and it wasn't quite that —" Malone shakes their head. "I recognized some of the words, but —"

"Yiddish," Noah says, gulping down his dread. "It was Yiddish."

"I didn't know you speak Yiddish," Malone says wonderingly. Just then, Sergeant Levin pulls up to the doors in a golf cart.

"What's going on here?" Her eyes scan Pulaski, Malone, and Elena, then focus in recognition on Noah. Her lips tighten into a scowl. "Why'd you detain these people?"

"They were trying to break in." Pulaski gestures at Noah with his nightstick. "This one had some kind of fit."

"They live inside," Sergeant Levin shakes her head. "You don't remember this kid? You tackled him a few weeks back." She unclips a key ring from her belt loop, unlocks the arena doors, and holds one open for Elena. "Ma'am."

Pulaski hocks up a wad of spit and launches it at the ground, then heads back into the tent city. His uniform is back to solid blue.

As Noah passes, Sergeant Levin catches his wrist. "Hey, are you alright? Do you need a doctor?"

He should probably say yes, but the last thing he wants is to explain what a dybbuk is to one of the Red Cross doctors.

With his luck, it'd be the same one who misgendered him on his first day in the arena. He shakes his head.

"Well, don't get caught out after curfew again," Sergeant Levin warns. "Y'all're lucky I was on duty tonight."

Malone and Elena pepper him with questions on the walk back to the cots. "I get fits like that sometimes," he lies, shrugging off their questions. "It's fine. I just need to get some sleep."

Malone wants him to see the on-call doctor, but again he refuses. "Where'd you learn Yiddish?" they ask suspiciously.

"My grandmother," he says, and this is not entirely a lie. Sometimes, when she would babysit, Yetta would talk on the phone with her sisters in Yiddish. Maybe he'd absorbed some of that language and stored it deep in the recesses of his memory. Maybe there's still a rational, DSM-V-approved explanation for what happened here.

But the sentence, "Xenoglossia was a certain sign of possession" keeps playing in his mind. His heart seizes up when he recalls Abe's pale face so close to, and then melding into his own. Is the ghost still inside his skin? Could he take control again at any moment?

Noah boots up his computer and searches his books and articles for exorcism instructions. King David's trick of using music hadn't worked, but recreating a medieval exorcism seems impossible. First off, he needs a minyan — a group of ten Jewish men — then holy amulets, a shofar, incense, potions with ingredients he's never heard of. Hoping these props are just nice-to-haves, he skims to the actual ceremony — here, the rabbi in charge commands the dybbuk to speak and reveal who it had been in life. Then there's a lot of chanting — invoking different names of God, reciting verses of the Talmud forward, backward, and sideways. Noah's mind catches on one line from Hayyim Vital's account — the rabbi whose wife had a "male soul" —

At the conclusion of each round, say with strength, "Depart, depart quickly!" ... everything depends on your firming and strengthening your heart like a mighty one, with no fear, and let your heart not soften, or he will become stronger and not heed your words.

Later, as he tries to fall asleep, listening to the coughs of smoke-filled lungs echo down the promenade, Noah squeezes his eyes tight, probing the corners of his mind for any alien presence. But if Abe is there, he doesn't want to be found, and Noah falls asleep to that three word-refrain echoing in his mind:

Depart, depart quickly!

The next morning, everyone lines up for breakfast as usual, but the steamer trays remain empty. A few Red Cross employees huddle together behind the tables, then disappear up the stairs to the administrative offices. After an hour, the people in line start shouting, and the cop on duty send everyone back to their cots. Stomach growling, Noah heads to his usual volunteer meetup, but no one else shows.

Back at Montrose Dos, Malone is tweeting their outrage over the food shortage. "People can't get food all over the city. Restaurants are closed. There's been another run on grocery stores." They hold up their phone to show a video of two women brawling over a box of hamburger helper. "The Ardmore and Texarkana fires are blocking delivery trucks from Oklahoma. And of course nothing's coming from the south or west. The governor says a convoy of food trucks is on its way ... escorted by the national guard." Malone falls silent, scrolling. "People are acting like *we're* to blame for the food shortage. There's all these nasty memes about Houston people and Austin people, and ... Oh my god!"

Noah peers over their shoulder and sees that meme of Cary Grant pointing at a door, captioned with, "*Get out, Austin queers.*" Someone else has tweeted a gif of someone getting punched with "#RealDallasites *Take out Houston trash.*"

Noah feels sick. "Aren't these the same people who were falling all over themselves to donate to you a few weeks ago?"

"The mayor is feeding this," Malone says. "He says the federal government should ship us out to other states. And the press isn't helping. There was this article yesterday about how filthy it's gotten in the arena, with all these pictures of the graffiti. They care more about their precious arena than, like, their fellow human beings."

"Y'all were babies, but the same thing happened in Houston, when all those folks came to the Astrodome, after Hurricane Katrina hit New Orleans," Elena says. "People's racist side came out real quick. The news kept talking about a 'crime wave,' and a bunch of white people were lobbying the mayor to kick out all the refugees."

Noah snorts bitterly. "And now those people are in the same spot. Don't these Dallas folks see it could happen to them here, just as easily?"

"That's the last thing they want to see," Elena says. "Being cruel to us? That's how they prove they're still in control."

🕊

There's no lunch that day either. Noah's stomach growls, and soon food is all he can think about. There's little movement in the arena, with everyone sticking to their cots to conserve energy. They're all just waiting. Noah wonders what'll happen when their patience runs out.

At last, a big Sysco truck pulls into the delivery yard behind the arena. Noah rushes to volunteer unloading the pallets of food. Bags of chicken stew are slashed open and dumped into steamer trays. The cops have to shout and hold out their arms to prevent a stampede at the food line.

Noah unloads crate after crate of food. Seemingly a huge amount, but it'll last a few days at most. Maybe by then, the fires will have died down, and regular deliveries will be able to get through. But what has the drought and all these fires done to the nation's crops? What happens if there's no more food to load on the trucks? Noah pushes the thought away, determined to enjoy this meal while he can. As he joins the back of the food line, the phone in his pocket buzzes. An unknown number.

"Hello," a man says. "I'm trying to reach Nora Mishner?"

A few weeks ago, Noah might've hung up at the sound of his old name. But now, it means someone from the past, someone who might know his parents.

"This is, um ..." He clears his throat and raises the pitch of his voice. "That's me."

"Nora, my name is Saul Cohen. I'm your father's attorney. I'm calling because rescue workers accessed your parents' home several days ago, and ..." He pauses, searching for words. Noah's throat tightens, knowing what's coming already. "I'm so sorry, Nora. Your parents did not survive the flood."

Noah doesn't cry. He feels nothing at all, as if a powerful wind has blown away all the matter filling his skin, leaving nothing but empty air. This is shock, he supposes. He takes a step forward in the food line.

"I'm sorry to be the one to bear this news."

"Okay. Thank you for telling me," Noah says, eager to get off the phone. He doesn't feel like unpacking his grief for this perfect stranger.

"Wait — I know this is a shock, but we have some things to discuss. Your parents left a will. They want to be cremated, so you'll need to arrange that, and perhaps a memorial service? And ... well, you know your father had considerable financial assets. And you're his primary beneficiary."

Noah sits on his cot, bolting down his food without tasting it. Maybe the phone call wasn't real — maybe it was a hunger-induced hallucination. He logs into his bank account on his phone, though, and sees more digits there than ever before. Saul had explained that this is a preliminary transfer of his parent's liquid assets. There's much more to come — trusts, property, mutual funds. Noah knows he was raised in privilege, but he had no idea his father had accumulated *this* much. Maybe he should've guessed. His dad spent forty years in oil and gas, working for the petrochemical companies that extracted the fuel that warmed the globe and caused the storm that drowned him.

The thought of it makes Noah sick, and he feels a wild impulse to call up Saul and give the money back. But of course he won't. Because money is money, and those digits in his bank account are the closest thing he'll ever feel to a hug from his father again. He'll take it as proof that his parents had wanted back into his life, eventually — they'd just run out of time.

Elena is painting Malone's nails in a soft grey color, silhouetted against the bathroom door, where a pink slur still bleeds through the white paint. First things first, Noah will use the money to get his friends the hell out of here. He hasn't told them about the money yet. Partly because he's ashamed of it. And partly because if he tells them about the money, he'll have to tell them about his parents, and that will make their deaths incontrovertibly real. He can't afford to deal with grief until they are all far away from this place.

He spends the rest of his laptop's battery charge reading news reports from around the country, trying to figure out where they should go. The western US is burning. He doesn't want to live anywhere near a coast. The Mississippi is also flooded, the worst it's been in a hundred years, and there are food shortages everywhere. They could try for Canada, but it's getting harder for Americans to cross the border. Right-wing Canadian politicians are even talking about building a wall.

Malone and Elena fall asleep while he's still bathed in the glow of his screen. He tries to buy plane tickets to Toronto using multiple airlines, then Chicago, then New York, but all the flights are full. He reads about the rush on the Dallas airport, sees pictures of the crowds choking the terminals, the lines of cars, stretching for miles down the highway. Everyone is trying to get the hell out of Texas.

It seems like their best bet is to get to the Greyhound station in the morning and try to catch a bus or a ride-share headed out of state, to somewhere the airports are still functioning. At two in the morning, he decides to try for sleep. He slips his laptop in his backpack, curls around the bag, and dozes off.

Shhhhh!

Abe leans over him, holding a finger to grey lips. Noah's heart slams in his chest.

"What now?" he whispers.

The ghost boy backs up, beckoning with a pale hand. Groaning with reluctance, Noah shoulders his backpack and follows. At least the dybbuk is outside his body.

Abe leads him up the stairs to the second level smoker's balcony. The night sky is brightened by an orange glow, and the air tastes of ash, as usual. But tonight, the fires burn closer — a few blocks away, a column of black smoke churns into the sky from behind tall buildings. Sirens mingle with screams — and some are coming from the edge of the tent city, where a crowd of people have gathered around one of the tents. It's swaying back and forth, like a vast animal settling on its haunches, then it falls. People scatter in every direction — an ant pile after it's stepped on.

"What's going on?" Noah asks, and to his surprise, the ghost answers.

"They don't want you in their city," Abe says, nodding to the mob that has set to tearing down another tent.

"Why isn't anyone stopping them?" Noah scans the crowd for officer Pulaski or Sergeant Levin, but finds no flashes of navy uniforms in the crowds below. The cops are gone, and though he was afraid of them, their sudden absence sends him into a panic.

Abe points around the curve of the arena to the north doors, where a clump of men have gathered. One is hurling a metal trash can into the bulletproof glass doors, and another is cracking at it with a baseball bat. Standing at the edges, shouting with approval, is a slight, hunched man with a shock of white hair. Roger Thibodeaux and all his new friends are trying to bust into the arena. Slung over all their shoulders are long, black guns.

Noah doesn't need to ask how they got them. This is Texas, after all, where AR-15s practically grow on trees. Of course those men have found a way to arm themselves. Maybe they're breaking into the arena to steal food, or maybe they have violence in mind. Noah isn't going to stick around to find out.

Beside him, Abe crouches over a long, green bag, the length of a man. He holds open the drawstring top, and pitch blackness yawns within.

"There's only room for one!" Abe hisses.

Then he and the duffel vanish. There's a fire escape ladder where the ghost stood a moment before, dropping down to the pavement behind the dumpsters.

Noah understands what Abe wants him to do. He is not supposed to go back for Malone, who can't shut up in the face of injustice. He is not supposed to go back for Elena, who can't pass as anyone Roger Thibodeaux wouldn't hate. "There's only room for one" means he will sneak past the angry mobs much easier by going it alone.

All his worldly possessions are already on his back, and his bank account is flush. He could slip down the ladder, slip past the mobs, slip out of Texas.

Wood cracks on thick glass. The Nazis are at the door. An instinct honed from millions of years of evolution and thousands of years of persecution screams *go, go — GO!*

He fights it. He imagines Malone and Elena sleeping on their cots in the darkened promenade below. He can't — he *won't* abandon his friends again. With a great effort of will, he wrenches himself away from the fire escape, grabs the door handle, and heads back inside the arena. He flies down the stairs, taking them two at a time, but as soon as he reaches the ground floor, he freezes, arrested by the vision that greets him.

Gone are the concession stands, the posters of basketball players, the jumbled colors of peoples' belongings. The promenade is now a curving corridor of blank tile, and the cots have become steel hospital gurneys. On each one lies a corpse, skin bloated and blue, water still dripping from their lifeless fingers and the tips of their hair.

Abe stands among the gurneys, now a full-grown man, in a three-piece suit and a fedora. He holds a metal ruler in one fist and a long matchstick in the other. This is the Abe of Herschel's childhood — who beat him for his errors reading the Torah, the Abe who walked out on his family when his debts threatened ruin. "Go back," Abe growls, pointing the ruler at Noah's chest, "Or you'll die with these gentiles."

"Why are you doing this?" Noah shakes his head as if he can shake off the visions.

"You're the last of the Mishner family. You have to survive!"

"*They're* my family too," Noah says through gritted teeth, and he forces himself to walk down the rows of cots, searching the grotesquely distorted faces of the corpses for someone familiar. A line from his research catches in his mind. He squeezes his eyes shut tight. "Depart, depart quickly!" he whispers.

When he opens his eyes again, the drowned still stare blankly up at the ceiling. Abe smirks, "You can't get rid of me."

"Depart, depart quickly!" Noah repeats in a firmer voice. Abe only steps to one side, gesturing to the gurney behind him.

Two corpses lay on the narrow frame, holding each other in a last embrace. One of them wears a face Noah has only imagined, obscured beneath a thick beard. The other is a teenage girl in pressed powder, with pin curls set into her soft, black hair. They are Noah and Nora, and they are both so beautiful, even in death.

"They both die if you do," Abe says.

Somewhere ahead, glass shatters and skitters on tile. Roger's friends have broken through the inner doors.

Noah starts grabbing the cold, damp shoulders of corpses and shaking them, repeating the exorcism under his breath. One of these bodies must belong to Malone or Elena. If he can wake them up, maybe they'll pull him from this nightmare.

"If you won't go," Abe growls, raising the ruler overhead, "I'll make you!" He rushes at Noah, edges blurring. As the ghost crashes into him, icy plasma once again penetrates his skin and freezes his muscles. This time, Noah fights for control of his body. He's lost the power of speech, but his mind chants *Depart, depart quickly!* But the cold keeps spreading, flooding his fingertips and toes. Ice crystals spread at the edges of his vision. Then everything goes black, and he is falling —

He awakens in a circle of light, beyond which is darkness. An old man holds the source of the light — a burning torch. The man is bald, save for a fuzz of grey at his temples, and his eyes are ringed with deep wrinkles, set in a pattern of suffering.

"Where are we?" Noah asks. His thoughts are disjointed and foggy. Maybe he should've started with "Who am I" because he can't quite remember that either.

"This is Vilna, the shtetl where I grew up." The old man straightens as much as his stooped back will allow. "Get up now, the others are coming."

Noah picks himself up off the dirt. His eyes have adjusted to the darkness somewhat, and he can see the peaks of wooden houses lining the road, their boards rough and uneven — hand-hewn. From the pitch-darkness beyond, footsteps drum the earth, coming closer. The fear in the old man's voice catches in Noah's chest too, and he hurries to follow the old man.

As they flee, he can't shake the feeling that something isn't right. There was something he was trying to do — something important. And who is this old man, exactly? Noah's never seen him before, yet there's something familiar in the man's gait. And with every step they take down the packed-dirt road, the prickling at the back of his neck intensifies. He's certain they're headed in the wrong direction.

My friends!" he blurts, clinging to a sudden scrap of memory. "We were in the arena. I was trying to get back to my friends — "

"They are already lost," Abe says, without breaking his stride.

"You're Abe too," Noah says, slowing to a halt. "The Abe my father met, in the cigar store. You didn't recognize your own son ..."

Abe waves him on urgently. "We must hurry!"

The footsteps beat louder at Noah's back, and he glances over his shoulder. He can make out figures in the distance now, holding torches of their own, but he cannot see the faces of his pursuers.

"No ..." Noah says, taking a step backwards. "No, you abandoned your family. I'm not like that!"

"You think you're so different?" Abe turns to him, smirking. "Tell me, when was the last time you saw your parents? And those friends you lived with — the *feygelehs* — when I brought you out of the flood, you left them behind to drown." He laughs cruelly, and his hand flicks between Noah's chest and his own. "No, no — you and me — we're the same."

Grief floods through Noah, weighing him to the ground. The old man is right. His parents, his friends — he left them all behind, and now they are lost to him forever.

The approaching footsteps thunder in his ears. Whoever they are — gentiles out on pogrom, Nazis, Roger Thibodeaux and his friends — they are right at his heels. If he doesn't run now, they will have him.

Abe stretches out a hand, eyes pleading. "Come."

"No," Noah whispers. "I'm *not* like you. I won't let all my stories be about the people I left behind."

Turning his back on Abe, Noah steps into the darkness.

At first, all he can see is the light of their torches. He heads back up the road towards them, expecting rough hands to seize him at any moment. Slowly, faces resolve beneath the flickering lights — faces he recognizes. His heart catches in his throat.

The first to emerge from the gloom is Yetta, in the navy, polka-dot dress she always wore to temple. Herschel holds a torch beside her, looking as he did in Noah's furthest-back memory, hearty and red-cheeked, before his eyes grew sunken from the chemo.

"Look at your beard!" his grandfather says wonderingly, patting Noah's cheek. "Almost as good as mine."

"In my day girls didn't grow beards," Yetta says, but then she shrugs. "Ehh, but then, in my day, girls didn't do lots of things! So what do I know?"

Two more people step forward, and his breath catches. "You're here too?" he says, as his parents' faces resolve beneath the torchlight.

"Of course we are," says his mother, stretching out her arms.

A little-boy part of him wants to run forward, but it's been so long since his parents' love was something uncomplicated. He searches their faces for that familiar knot between their brows, that frown of disapproval that's marked their expressions towards him ever since he started making decisions for himself.

Instead, he finds that his parents, in their afterlife, seem freed from all parental expectations and disappointments. They look at him with wide-eyed rapture, like new parents holding a squalling infant in their arms.

They look at him like he's perfect.

Noah does rush forward then. His dad wraps an arm around his shoulders. His mother pats the back of his neck. "We're always with you, son."

"Like it or not, kid, you're stuck with us," says his dad.

Noah disentangles himself and looks back at the lone, bent figure, marooned in an island of light.

"Does that go for him too?"

"Unfortunately, yes," dad answers. "Abe will always be a part of you too."

"The schmuck!" Herschel snarls, spitting in Abe's general direction.

"But you don't have to listen to that old fart," comes another, achingly familiar voice, and three happy, young faces appear.

Noah squeals and rushes into Max, Emeric, and Sasha's arms. Instead of holding torches, their faces are illuminated with cell-phone lights.

"We got you, bish," Max says.

"We must stan," Emeric agrees solemnly, "eternally."

"I've missed y'all so much," Noah says. "I'm so sorry I left you during the storm."

Sasha smooths the hair back from his forehead. "We know. We can talk about that later."

"It's time to go back," his dad says, stepping forward again.

"Go get your friends," Sasha whispers. "I just love that Elena. I wish we could've all gone out dancing together."

"And Malone!" Emeric claps xer hands. "They're so fierce. I can't help crushing."

Beyond the circle of his family and friends, a huge crowd of people has gathered. Their faces are shadowed beneath stiff hats and headscarves, but he thinks he knows who they are. Great-great-grandmothers and great-great-great grandfathers, on and on, filling the road that stretches back into the village — way back, past the borders of Vilna and a hundred other shtetls, little villages strung along dirt roads winding all the way down the spine of the continent, all the way back to antiquity, to Israel, and further still — to the dawn of his people in the world. They come from times and places so distant, they can hardly understand Noah's choices, or the world he lives in. He baffles them, as each successive generation has baffled them. And yet, he senses an energy radiating out from them — a tangible feeling of goodwill that washes through his bones, setting his mind at peace. What he understands is this — they love him.

He turns one last time to Abe, who is scowling and muttering, off by himself. Even from him, Noah senses a flicker of that same warm energy. He doesn't tell Abe to "depart," because he understands now — there's no getting rid of an ancestor, unpleasant as they may be. But he has nothing to fear anymore from the old dybbuk. Somewhere far-off, sensation is returning to Noah's body. He feels the cold tile of the arena floor beneath his spine, and Vilna begins fading into pale mist.

"Thank you," he tells Abe, meaning it. Then he opens his eyes.

Elena and Malone lean over him, a crowd of their cot-neighbors gathered behind.

"Noah? Noah!" Malone says, hand to his forehead. "You did it again. You had one of those fits."

Elena nods, eyes wide with worry. "You were yelling — *Depart! Depart!* — And thrashing around. Woke us all up."

"This time you're *going* to see a doctor," Malone says.

But a *crack!* rings out from around the northern bend in the promenade. Glass skitters across concrete. The crowd around Noah freezes, heads whipping towards the noise.

"It's Thibodeaux and his friends," Noah says urgently. "I saw them — they've got guns."

People gasp, someone cries out. Elena and Malone help Noah to his feet, but the rest of the crowd are bolting. Some grab up their belongings, others take off running towards the southern doors. More cracks of gunfire rip through the air. Screams ring out from the basketball court and are picked up in a chorus all around them.

Elena looks desperately towards the southern doors, where a crush of people jam the promenade, trying to force their way through. "I know another way out," Noah says, praying that the fire escape Abe showed him was real and not another hallucination.

He leads Elena and Malone up the empty stairwell to the second floor. Out on the balcony, he unlatches the fire escape, sending up another thank-you to Abe, wherever the ghost boy is lurking. He waits, glancing nervously over his shoulder, as the others climb down the ladder, and then he too climbs to the chaotic streets below. They move quickly through shadows, leaving behind the arena that has become a kind of home, not knowing when or where they'll arrive at another. It is not the first home they've had to abandon, and it likely won't be the last. But they do not depart empty-handed. There is a shelter they carry between them, built in furtive glances, in waiting for Elena to catch up, panting, after sprinting past the dumpsters, in hands squeezed, crouched in an empty tent, waiting for the laughter of drunken men to dwindle.

Noah doesn't know if they'll make it through the city, past the mob, past police at war with looters, and so many armed, angry men. He doesn't know if his dad's money will save them, or if digits in a cloud are already worthless. He doesn't know when they'll find safety again, or if such a place even exists anymore. None of them know the rules of this brutal, new world, but they'll figure them out together.

Acknowledgments

I owe a debt of gratitude for the historical context of this book to J.H. Chajes's *Between Worlds: Dybbuks, Exorcists, and Early Modern Judaism,* Rachel Elior's *Dybbuks and Jewish Women in Social History, Mysticism, and Folklore,* and S. Ansky's *A Dybbuk, or Between Two Worlds.* I'm also deeply grateful for the revelatory insights of Rabbi David J. Meyer in his article, "What the Torah Teaches us about Gender Fluidity and Transgender Justice," found on the website Religious Action Center of Reform Judaism (the RAC).

Thank you to my editor at Stelliform Press, Selena Middleton, for believing in Noah right from the start. Thank you to my agent Kerstin Wolf and Bob DiForio for your support and guidance.

Everett Burge, sensitivity reader extraordinaire, thank you for helping me understand Noah, and myself, better than I could've done on my own.

Thank you to the amazing communities of trans and Jewish writers I've found on twitter, and to all my beta-readers: Daniel Delgado, Rowan Fae, Louis Evans, and Kevin Wilson.

The heart of this book comes from all the queer families I've found through the years, even before we knew ourselves — for Katie, Sydney and Adam, Sahra and Mary, Julien and Kyna, María-Elisa, and all the friends of Apricot Summers. And a particular thank-you to Aster, whose example gave me the courage to find myself.

Thank you, Dad, for teaching me how to tell a story, where to put a comma, and for being the first and biggest fan of my writing. Thank you Jessie, Seymour, Anna, Sarah, Hymen, and even that schmuck Abe, and all my ancestors going back, back, to the dawn of our people in the world. I know I must baffle you, but I hope you're proud nonetheless.

Thank you to Jeff & Linda and Rick & Myra for sharing your faith and Seders with my family over the years. Your loving examples showed me how beautiful our religious heritage can be.

This book would have been impossible without my husband Ike's love and support. Thank you for never expecting me to be anything other than *me*.

And to Ramona, may you inherit all of your ancestors' wisdom, minus the neuroses.

About the Author

I grew up in a more-rural-than-suburban town outside Chicago called St. Charles, where I was definitely the only queer Jewish kid in school — something which invited, uh, a *lot* of bullying over the years. Raised as an atheist, patrilineal Jew, my earliest memory of even being aware that I *was* Jewish was when I was about six years old, and a girl down the street told me we couldn't play together anymore because her dad said we were dirty Jews. Throughout my childhood, I was often called queer and Jewish slurs, harassed by neo-Nazi kids on the bus, had Swastikas drawn on my driveway and lockers, and was the target of rumors that my family ate babies or worshipped Satan, etc. etc.

All this trouble, and I never even got a gendered mitzvah party!

Luckily, my understanding of Judaism was not shaped by the more bigoted kids in my town. From my dad's side of the family and close friends, I learned that being Jewish was something to be proud of. I felt a lot of imposter-syndrome about my Jewishness, because we were atheists, because I was only half — but eventually I learned that Jewishness is an identity you can either be assigned or claim — an ineffable *something* that's very hard to define, yet permeates every aspect of your life — your language, jokes, even gestures. Kinda like — gee, I don't know — gender.

My great-grandfather's name was indeed Abraham Kern, and the stories about Abe in this book are grounded in truth, except for the bit about the duffel bag — that image occurred to me and I couldn't let it go. There's some familial compression here — it was actually Abe's father who taught my grandfather Seymour to read the Torah. He would indeed point to each letter with a matchstick and strangle and beat my grandfather for every mistake. My dad met his grandfather only once, in a cigar store, and I tried to recreate that story here just the way my dad tells it.

I have always been gender non-conforming and queer — something that my peers understood better than I did, even in the years I was trying hard as I could to fit in. After years of wishing that being trans "was a thing" when I was growing up, I finally came out as trans nonbinary at the age of 32, and my gender story is still evolving. Although Noah's feelings and gender struggles echo my own, I do not live as a trans man, and so I'm indebted to the help of my sensitivity reader, Everett Burge, for lending his perspective to this story.

Although I was born and raised a Midwesterner, I've spent half my life now in Houston, Texas, where there are more queer Jews than you might think! After graduating with a degree in creative writing from Oberlin College, I moved down here for a bad relationship. Stayed to get my teaching degree. Wound up getting stuck when I met my husband, Ike, who works for NASA — so there's no escaping Space City now! I love-hate Houston. Love the food, people, balmy winters, and the slivers of coastal prairie and wild bayous full of alligators. Hate the brutal summers that get worse with climate change, the fact that my living room floods at least once a year, and that the chemical refineries down the street are worsening my asthma.

Here in Houston, I've lived through Hurricane Ike, Hurricane Harvey, Tropical Storm Imelda, the Tax Day Flood, Memorial Day Flood, and too many minor floods to remember. The walls of our living room still show a band of unpainted drywall at the bottom, because why go through the trouble of painting when it's only a matter of time before we flood again? (Or at least, until we can afford to raise our foundation).

In 2009, the Addicks and Barker dams and reservoirs to the west of Houston were named by the Army Corps of Engineers to be at "extremely high risk of catastrophic failure." If either of these dams fail, projections are that the city, from Memorial to downtown, would be largely destroyed, with damage far more severe than what we sustained during Hurricane Harvey. Although the gates on both dams are currently being replaced, both reservoirs are still at risk of failure in a bad enough storm. A study that will make recommendations for more extensive repairs to the dams is ongoing and won't conclude until October 2021.

STELLIFORM
PRESS

**Earth-focused fiction. Stellar stories.
Stelliform.press.**

Stelliform Press is shaping conversations about
nature and our place within it. Check out our
upcoming titles and articles and leave a comment or
review on your favorite social media platform.